MURDER IN THE DARK

Star walked along the alley and was nearly to the street when she heard a slurred voice from the shadows.

"Hey girlie, How 'bout a little fun?"

Star was tired, but she was game. She never turned down an honest dollar, and this would be one she wouldn't have to share with Fanny Belle. So she walked over to where a dark figure leaned against the wall of a saloon that fronted on the street.

"What're you looking for?" she asked.

"Just a little fun, like I said."

"You have money?"

"Sure do."

Star wasn't stupid. "Let's see it."

A hand reached into a pocket and came out with a coin.

"I can't see it," Star said.

"Then come over here."

Star leaned forward. The knife was so sharp that she hardly felt it. . . .

The *Apache Law* series:
#1: THE LONELY GUN

Apache Law
Hellfire

Luke Adams

LEISURE BOOKS NEW YORK CITY

A LEISURE BOOK®

February 2000

Published by

Dorchester Publishing Co., Inc.
276 Fifth Avenue
New York, NY 10001

Copyright © 2000 by Dorchester Publishing Co., Inc.

ISBN 0-8439-4688-1

The name "Leisure Books" and the stylized "L" with design are trademarks of Dorchester Publishing Co., Inc.

Printed in the United States of America.

Hellfire

Chapter One

Mitch Frye was eating lunch with Jewel Reid when the two men walked up to the table and announced that they were going to kill him. Mitch finished chewing the bite of cornbread he'd just put into his mouth and then looked up at them.

"Why?" he asked.

"Because we don't like it that a goddamned Indian is sitting here with a white woman," one of the men said.

The large tent with the Eat Here sign out front went suddenly quiet. Only a second before, the tent had been filled with the hum of conversation and the sound of spoons clinking against bowls of stew. Now there was no sound at all except for the flapping of the canvas in the breeze.

The man who had spoken was short and wide, with a red face, small eyes that were set too close together, and a nose that looked as if someone had once hit it with a frying pan. He had a black beard, and lank black hair hung out from under his hat. He was holding a Colt's Peacemaker in his right hand, and it was pointed right at Mitch's belt buckle.

The short man's companion was a good foot taller than his friend. His arms hung down and ended in fists the size of saddlebags, and his wrists were as thick as Mitch Frye's ankles.

Mitch sighed. He didn't need trouble, not right now. He'd had a rough night that hadn't ended until well after midnight, and he didn't feel like getting involved in a fight. So he thought he'd try taking the easy way out.

"Indian bastard," the man said.

Well, Mitch thought, it was true. His mother had been a white woman, and his father had been an Apache. He'd never met his father, but he suspected that there was a strong family resemblance, since his appearance had caused him trouble often enough.

Not wanting trouble now, Mitch stood up and said, "You two are under arrest."

The short man grinned, revealing a set of teeth as ragged as the Rockies. "Who says?"

"I say," Mitch answered. "I'm the sheriff here in Paxton."

It was true. He hadn't asked to be the sheriff, he didn't want to be the sheriff, and he'd tried to get out of being the sheriff. But he was still the sheriff.

The big man laughed. "If you're the sheriff, I'm U.S. Grant. Where's your badge?"

"I don't have one. But I'm still the sheriff, even without it. Let's go, boys."

"What's the charge?" the smaller man asked.

Mitch thought for a second. "Disturbing the peace."

That brought a laugh from both men. Jewel Reid looked up at them and said, "He's not joking, you know."

The men stopped laughing and looked at her.

"Who asked you?" the tall one said. "A white woman that'd eat with an Indian, well, she ain't no better than she has to be, if you take my meaning. No better than a damn whore."

Mitch had been upset before, but the man's last statement made him angry. He didn't know why Jewel Reid liked him, but she did, in spite of her father's objections. And Mitch liked her, much to his own surprise. He'd never had a relationship with a woman before, except on a cash basis, and he didn't like it at all that the tall man was implying that he had a similar relationship with Jewel.

The short man waggled his pistol. "Ma'am," he said, "we don't care whether he's the sheriff or not. We're gonna kill him just the same."

"I don't think so," she said, and stabbed him in the thigh with her fork.

The man yelped in surprise, and Mitch slapped the hand that held the pistol. The Colt went off and sent a bullet over the heads of the diners and out the side of the tent.

The big man made a jump for Mitch, but he was a fraction of a second too late. Mitch had his own pistol out by that time, and he backhanded the man across the nose. There was a spurt of blood and a satisfying crunch, and the man fell to his knees. He put his hands to his face and said, "You broke my nose, you son of a bitch."

Mitch brought the pistol barrel down hard on top of the man's head to shut him up. He fell forward on his face and lay still.

When Mitch turned to the other man, he saw that Jewel had already taken care of him. She had thrown stew in his face and then cracked him on the cheekbone with the bowl, causing him to drop his pistol, which Jewel had picked up. She was now pointing it at his head.

"Thanks," Mitch said.

He wasn't used to having a woman help him out, but Jewel had already proved to him that she wasn't like any other woman he'd ever had dealings with. He wasn't surprised that she could take care of herself.

"What are we going to do with them?" Jewel asked.

"Take them to the jail. If you'll keep the gun on Shorty, I'll drag his friend along."

"Sounds like a good idea to me," Jewel said. "Move it out, Shorty."

"My name's not Shorty."

"What is it, then?" Mitch asked.

"Herman. Herman Tolliver."

Mitch looked at the man on the ground. "What about your friend?"

"That's Sam Spivey."

"All right, Herman," Mitch said. "I can't say I'm pleased to make your acquaintance."

He stooped down and slipped Spivey's pistol from its holster and stuck it in his belt. Then he grabbed Spivey's ankles and started dragging him through the tent. The talking and eating resumed, with several pointed remarks being directed toward Herman, who did his best to ignore them.

"You could at least turn him over," Herman said. "His face is messed up enough as it is."

Mitch kept right on going. "He should have thought of that before you two decided to kill me."

Ellie West, the owner of the establishment, stopped Mitch and Jewel at the door. "You want me to send you something over to the jail? You two hardly got started eating."

Mitch got free meals as part of his salary, but he didn't feel like eating anymore. So he said, "No, thanks. I'm much obliged to you, but I'll just wait till suppertime."

"All right," Ellie said. "I appreciate it that you didn't let those two do any damage to the place."

Mitch didn't see that there was much damage that could be done to a place like the Eat Here, but he said, "Just part of the job."

He dropped one of Spivey's legs and touched the brim of his hat. Then he picked up the leg and resumed his dragging.

The jail was right in back of Mitch's office and living quarters. There was nothing very fancy in Paxton, a mining boomtown that had sprung up practically overnight on the side of the mountain where it was located, but the jail was new and sturdy, and it sure beat chaining prisoners to a log, which was what Mitch had done previously.

Mitch dumped Spivey in the cell, and Jewel marched Tolliver in behind them. Mitch backed out and slammed the door.

"How long you planning to keep us in here?" Tolliver asked.

"Until I let you out," Mitch told him.

"When will that be?"

"I haven't decided yet."

"Goddamn it, you can't do that. What about a judge?"

"We don't have a judge in Paxton yet," Mitch said, turning to leave.

Tolliver was yelling something at his back, but Mitch paid no attention. He no longer cared what the man had to say. Not that he'd cared overmuch to begin with.

"You'd better take care of this," Jewel said. "It's a little too much gun for me."

Mitch took the pistol from her.

11

"I know what you're thinking," she said. "You're thinking that if I hadn't been with you, those men wouldn't have caused all that trouble."

"That's not what I was thinking," Mitch lied.

They went into his office, and he put the pistol in his desk. He didn't want to talk to Jewel about what had happened. He'd faced things like that all his life, and while they still bothered him, they weren't unexpected. Jewel, on the other hand, wasn't used to them, and he didn't want her to be.

"I'm a grown woman," Jewel said. "I can associate with anyone I want to. What happened back there doesn't bother me."

"It bothers me," said a voice from the doorway.

Jewel and Mitch looked to see Jewel's father, J. Paxton Reid, standing there. Reid was a heavyset man, red-faced and balding. He was also the founder of Paxton, the owner of the biggest mine in the vicinity, and the town's mayor. He was the man who had tricked Mitch into signing a false confession of murder and forced him to take the sheriff's job.

For obvious reasons, Mitch wasn't too fond of him.

"What are you doing here?" Mitch asked him.

"I heard about what happened at Ellie West's place, and I came over to see if my daughter was all right. I don't like it when she's involved in things like that."

"I can take care of myself," Jewel said. "You don't have to worry about me."

"I do worry about you, though," Reid said. He looked at Mitch. "And about who you spend your time with."

"I'll be glad to turn in my resignation and get out of your town," Mitch said. "All you have to do is ask. In fact, you don't even have to ask. I'll give it to you right now."

"I didn't say I wanted you to leave, so don't start talking about resignations. I thought you were the right man for this job when I hired you, and I still think so. But I don't want my daughter getting hurt."

Jewel had helped Mitch solve a series of murders that had begun with a miner getting his head bashed in. Reid hadn't liked it at all that his daughter had been involved in a murder investigation.

"She's not the one who got hurt," Mitch said. "You should see the two men in the jail back there."

"That's beside the point. My daughter was exposed to danger because she was eating lunch with you."

"I eat with whoever I please," Jewel said.

Mitch was both pleased and disturbed by her words. Jewel was a beautiful woman, and it was clear that she liked him. He did not know exactly where their relationship was going to develop, and he was a little afraid to find out, but it was obviously going to be interesting.

Reid looked at his daughter for a second or two, then walked out of the office and into the street.

"Did you really mean that about your resignation?" Jewel asked when her father had gone.

Mitch had never told her about how he'd become the sheriff, and he was sure Reid hadn't told her, either.

"I meant it," he said. "But it doesn't have anything to do with you."

"I hope not," Jewel said. She looked at Mitch. "I suppose I'd better go on back to work." She worked in Reid's office as a bookkeeper. She was very good at her job. That was another of the things Mitch admired about her. "Don't let my father bother you. He's really not as bad as he seems."

"Maybe not," Mitch said, but he didn't really believe it.

Chapter Two

Later that afternoon, Mitch went to check on Tolliver and Spivey. Tolliver was still yelling that Mitch couldn't keep them in jail without letting them go before a judge. Spivey wasn't saying anything. He was sitting on a cot and leaning back against the wall. His nose sat a little crooked on his face, and it was clotted with blood and dirt.

"You don't look too good," Mitch told him.

"And whose fault is that, you Indian son of a bitch?" Tolliver asked. "It's a wonder you didn't kill him, dragging him in the street like you did."

Mitch gave Tolliver a long look. "I'll tell you who I'd like to kill."

Tolliver decided to shut up. He lay down on his cot and turned his face to the wall.

"Let's see about that nose," Mitch said to Spivey.

He walked over to the man, and before Spivey could object, Mitch grabbed his nose and twisted

15

it sharply. There was a quiet *crack*, and Spivey yowled.

"That looks a lot better," Mitch said. "It's more or less back where it belongs now. Sort of matches your partner's. If you stay out of trouble, I think it'll heal up just fine."

"You're gonna pay for that, you bastard," Tolliver said without looking around.

"We'll see," Mitch told him.

He stood there watching them while he rolled himself a cigarette, which he lit with a match from his pocket. Neither of them seemed to have anything more to say.

"I'm going over to eat supper now," Mitch told them. "I know it's a little early, but someone interrupted my lunch. I'll bring you boys back something if I get the chance."

Nobody said anything, so Mitch left them there.

Paxton had more miners than Mitch could count, three saloonkeepers, a newspaper editor, and an abundance of whores, but it didn't have a church. It looked as if that was about to change.

Mitch pulled a handbill off the post in front of the Eat Here tent and looked at it. It said:

COME ONE, COME ALL
BE SAVED, HEALED, AND SATISFIED
HEAR THE WORD OF THE LORD
PREACHED FOR SINNERS
SING THE SONGS OF PRAISE
IN THE BIG TENT SOUTH OF TOWN
THE REVEREND DEUCE DAVIS IN THE PULPIT
SERVICES BEGIN 30 MINUTES AFTER SUNDOWN

No one would have any trouble finding the tent, Mitch thought. There was only one road leading into Paxton from the bottom of the mountain, and you had to take the same road out unless you wanted to go right on up to the top. And after you got there, there was nowhere to go but back down by that very same route.

Mitch folded the handbill and walked over to Harvey Radin's newspaper office. Radin had set up his press in a building that someone had built with the intention of starting a butcher shop. The shop hadn't worked out, so the building had been available for Paxton's first newspaper.

When Mitch walked into the office, Radin was there, but so was J. Paxton Reid. Mitch wasn't surprised. Reid had a way of turning up when Mitch wasn't expecting him. But it was just as well he was there.

"Did you print this handbill?" Mitch asked Radin, holding it out to him.

Radin was a smooth-faced, medium-size man who wore a bowler hat. He must have liked the hat because he seldom removed it, even when he was inside or working on his newspaper.

He glanced at the handbill. "I printed it, all right. First job this morning. I see that the reverend has already been putting them out where people can see them." He paused. "I don't think he'd appreciate it if he knew you were pulling them down."

"I just took the one," Mitch said. "What's he like?"

"The reverend? Well, he's tall—taller than you. Dresses all in black, or at least that's how he was dressed this morning. Not a bad-looking man, if you like the sour type."

Reid took the handbill from Mitch and read it. Then he handed it back to the sheriff.

"Deuce," Reid said. "Funny kind of a name for a preacher. A gambler, now, it might make more sense."

"It doesn't have anything to do with cards," Radin said. "I guess you'd have to see him to understand."

"Why don't you tell us," Mitch suggested.

"It's his hand," Radin said. "His left hand. He just has two fingers on it, unless you count his thumb, which I guess he doesn't. He claims that he had a little run-in with a grizzly up on the Yellowstone River one time. There was a disagreement about which one of them was going to eat the trout Davis had caught, and it got a little heated."

"You said *claims*," Mitch pointed out. "Does that mean you don't believe him?"

"He's a preacher," Radin said. "So I guess he's telling the truth. Still . . ."

"Still, what?

"Well, he doesn't look like the kind of a man that would get into any argument with a bear. He's thin as a hitch rail."

"If he'd lie about that, he'd lie about other things," Mitch said.

"I didn't say he was lying," Radin said, though he still looked a little doubtful. "He probably wasn't."

Mitch folded the handbill and put it in his pocket. "Sounds to me like you talked to him for a good while."

"A newspaperman is always looking for stories," Radin said. "You can read all about the reverend in this week's paper if you've a mind to."

"What I'm wondering about is why a preacher would want to come to a place like Paxton," Mitch said.

"What do you mean by that?" Reid asked.

"No offense," Mitch said. "I know it's your town and you're proud of it. But look at it from a preacher's point of view. What is there here for him? This is a boomtown. There aren't any families here to speak of, just a bunch of hard-rock miners with most of the bark knocked off. They don't seem like a churchgoing bunch to me. For a church, you need women and kids. The women can generally make the men and the kids go, even if they don't much like it. But I can't see these miners going on their own."

"That just shows you don't know much about miners," Reid said. "Or about towns like this one. I expect that tent will be just about full. Tell him, Radin."

Radin rubbed his beardless chin. "Mr. Reid's right. What is there to do in this place after a hard day's work, Mr. Frye?"

Mitch could answer that one without thinking. "Gambling, drinking, and whoring. Which is what most people seem to be interested in. They don't have a lot in common with going to a preaching."

"It might be hard for you to believe," Radin said, "but people get tired of gambling, drinking, and whoring after a while. Even the kind of men you find in a mining town. They're looking for something different, something that will entertain them. This preacher might be just the thing."

"Well," Reid said. "I guess it couldn't hurt to have a preacher around. It might make your job a little easier, Sheriff."

Mitch nodded. "It might, at that," he said.

But he didn't believe it for a minute.

Mitch carried two bowls of stew and some cornbread back to the jail for Tolliver and Spivey, both of whom ate in sullen silence. Mitch watched them for a minute or two, then went back to his office and smoked a cigarette. When he judged that they were about finished, he returned for the bowls.

"I'll tell you what, boys," he said. "I think we can strike a bargain so you two can get out of here in just a little while."

Both men looked at him with interest.

"What kind of a bargain would that be?" Tolliver asked, considerably less belligerent than he'd been earlier.

"I'll turn you loose if you'll go to church with me," Mitch said.

"Church?" Spivey said. "There ain't no goddamn church within fifty miles of this godforsaken town."

"There is now," Mitch said, and he told them about the Reverend Deuce Davis.

"I don't know," Tolliver said. "I'm not much for those hellfire-and-damnation preachers. They give me the fantods."

"That's 'cause you've never been baptized, you old reprobate," Spivey said. He tried to look pious, which wasn't easy considering the state of his nose. "My mama had me baptized when I wasn't but eight years old."

"For all the good it did," Tolliver said.

Spivey stood up, and Mitch got the impression that he was about to give his friend an un-Christian punch in the face.

"I think a nice long sermon would do the both of you some good," Mitch said. "But it's up to you. Either you go, or you spend the night in here."

Tolliver looked at Spivey, who nodded slightly.

"We'll go, then," Tolliver said.

"I think you've made the right decision," Mitch told them. "Maybe you'll learn a little something about brotherly love."

Mitch didn't really think they'd learn a thing,

but he figured that spending some time in the company of a hellfire preacher was a suitable punishment for their transgressions.

"I'll come to get you a little after sundown," he said.

It turned out that Reid and Radin were right. Mitch and his former prisoners found themselves among quite a crowd as they walked toward the outskirts of town. Most of the crowd was made up of the miners, but Mitch was surprised to see a couple of women that he'd never seen around town before. Obviously they were miners' wives, but they'd kept themselves pretty well out of sight until now. There were also a few other women in the crowd, but Mitch had seen them in the course of making his rounds. They worked for a woman who called herself Fanny Belle and who had set up a whorehouse in a tent near one of the saloons. There were a couple of other houses in town, but Mitch didn't see any of their girls. They were probably all working too hard to take time off for a sermon.

Jewel was there, too. She was one of the few young, eligible women in town, and the only reason she wasn't mobbed by suitors was the fact that she was Reid's daughter. The miners knew their coarse attentions wouldn't be welcome, and they kept well away from Jewel for the most part. When they did say anything at all to her, they were full of exaggerated politeness and respect.

Mitch wondered, not for the first time, why Reid allowed his daughter to stay in town. She could have gone back east and made a good life for herself with some respectable man of business. But maybe that wasn't the kind of life she wanted. Maybe she wanted the kind of independence she could never have back east. And maybe that explained her interest in Mitch, who believed that people were entitled to live however they pleased.

Mitch decided to turn his mind to other things. Thinking about Jewel always seemed to make him uncomfortable.

"I didn't think of you as much of a churchgoer," she said to him.

"Curiosity," Mitch said. "I'm always interested in hearing what people believe in."

Mitch himself didn't believe in much of anything. He'd been raised by his white mother, but she hadn't been a religious person. Considering the way the good people of the town treated her, Mitch could understand why. They hadn't treated him any better. Worse, if anything. He'd always wondered how someone could go to church on Sunday morning and sing songs about love and forgiveness and then go out and kick around the kid they called "half-breed" the same afternoon.

As for Mitch's father, well, Mitch had never seen him. And he really had no notion of what the Apache religion might be like. If the whites didn't like Mitch, the Apaches absolutely despised him.

"Are you a believer?" Mitch asked Jewel.

"I'm not sure," she said. "It sounds good, but it doesn't always seem to work out so well in practice."

Mitch said that he knew what she meant.

When they got to the lantern-lit tent, Mitch told his erstwhile prisoners that they were on their own, as long as they stayed for the whole service.

"Don't let me catch you trying to sneak out," he warned them. "I'll have my eye on you."

"We'll stay," Tolliver assured him, though he had a shifty look in his eye. "Ain't that right, Sam?"

Spivey nodded but didn't speak. He was looking into the tent as if reluctant to enter.

"You two go on in," Mitch said. "I'll just wait here till you've found a place."

Tolliver and Spivey looked around, but there was no getting away. They were hemmed in on all sides by the crowd. So they reluctantly entered the tent.

"What about you?" Jewel asked Mitch. "Are you really going to stay?"

"I guess so. I can make my rounds after it's over."

"Let's find a seat, then," Jewel said.

They went inside the tent. There were rows of improvised benches made from rough boards laid across boxes and barrels. Many of the seats were already taken, though some of the more hesitant members of the assembly were standing in the rear of the tent as if they had no intention of sitting. That was where Tolliver and Spivey had taken up their positions.

"Save me a seat," Mitch told Jewel.

He walked over to where Tolliver and Spivey stood. "I want you two to find some seats right down front. That way I can see you better."

The two men grumbled, but they moved away. Mitch waited until they'd found seats in the second row before joining Jewel.

There was a murmur of anticipation in the crowd, and before too long the Reverend Deuce Davis walked out to stand behind the makeshift pulpit at the front of the tent. He was as tall as Radin had described him, still dressed all in black. In his maimed left hand he carried a black Bible. There was one thing that Radin had neglected to mention, and that was the scar that ran from the corner of Davis's left eye all the way down the side of his jaw. Maybe that was another souvenir from his run-in with the grizzly, Mitch thought.

Davis looked out over the crowd without saying a word. He waited until the tent was absolutely silent, and then he began singing a song that started off with something about crossing a golden river called the Great Forever. He had a high, clear voice, and before he'd sung an entire verse, several of the miners had joined in. By the time he got to the chorus, more than half the crowd was singing along. More of them had been to church at one time or another than Mitch would have guessed.

Other songs followed, with the crowd showing more and more enthusiasm. Mitch had to admit the tunes were catchy. He might have joined in himself if he'd known any of the words, which of course he didn't.

Jewel did, however, and he enjoyed listening as her pure soprano soared above the other voices.

After six or eight songs, the Reverend Davis opened his Bible and looked out over the congregation for a moment. Then he said, "My text tonight is Proverbs, chapter seven. Hear the word of the Lord: 'And, behold, he met there a woman with the attire of a harlot, and subtle of heart. She is loud and stubborn; her feet abide not in her house: now is she without, now in the streets, and lieth in wait at every corner.'"

Davis paused and looked up. Everyone sat so quietly that Mitch wasn't sure that anyone except him was even breathing.

With a satisfied look, Davis resumed his reading. "'With her much fair speech she caused him to yield, with the flattering of her lips she forced him. He goeth after her straightway, as an ox goeth to the slaughter, or as a fool to the correction of the stocks; till a dart strike through his liver; as a bird hasteth to the snare, and knoweth not it is for his life. Hearken unto me now therefore, O ye children, and attend to the words of my mouth. Let not thine heart decline to her ways, go not astray in her paths. For she hath cast down many wounded: yea, many strong men have been slain by her. Her house is the way to hell, going down to the chambers of death.' "

Davis closed the Bible and laid it aside. "Friends, I am here to tell you tonight about the fiery pit that awaits any man who consorts with harlots. The wages of sin is death, and the difference between God and anybody else who might be paying your wages is that God is never going to cheat you. You're going to get everything you deserve, the full measure, and maybe more.

"You think I don't know what goes on in a town like this? Oh, you'd be wrong about that, brothers. I know, all right, and what's more, God knows. He knows the number of the very hairs on your heads, and if he knows that, don't you think he knows how you spend your time? Let me read you something again: 'Her *house* is the way to *hell*, going *down* to the chambers of *death*!' Now I don't think it could be any plainer than that, could it? The book says it's the way to *hell*, and that's exactly what it means. You're on the way to burning in a lake of eternal fire if you follow that road."

"You're right, brother," a woman called out. It wasn't one of the women who worked for Fanny Belle, Mitch noted.

"God knows I'm right," Davis shouted. He brandished the Bible. "God knows I'm right because it's his word that I'm reading to you. And a man that lies with harlots is like a bird that hasteth to the snare, and his death is just as sure!"

25

Someone shouted "Amen!" and the crowd began to stir. Mitch could see that things were going to get lively. But he found that he really didn't care. Maybe he wasn't as hard up for entertainment as some people, or maybe he just didn't like the idea of someone trying to tell him what to do. He couldn't make up his mind. But he could make up his mind to leave.

He started to rise, but Jewel reached out and plucked his shirtsleeve. He sat back down, and she leaned over to him.

"What's the rush?" she whispered in his ear. "Trying to leave before he passes the plate?"

Mitch knew the plate passing would commence sooner or later, but that wasn't why he was leaving.

"Have to make my rounds," he said.

"Maybe I'll see you later, then."

Mitch nodded, though he doubted it. He and Jewel didn't keep the same kind of company, not after dark.

As he left the tent, trying to be as inconspicuous as possible, Mitch looked around. There were several people he knew in the congregation. Sam Neely, who owned the combination livery stable and blacksmith shop where Mitch kept his horse, was there. J. Paxton Reid was standing near the back, listening intently. Radin was there, taking notes. Maybe he was planning to write up the sermon for the *Gazette*. Bill Carson, the manager of Reid's mine, was there, as was George Kelley, the owner of the town's bank. Even Ellie West was there. Mitch wondered who was running the Eat Here.

He didn't wonder long. He walked out into the cool night air, took a deep breath, and walked back up the road into town. He had to check out the saloons and make sure no one was trying to shoot up the town. It wouldn't hurt to walk by the bank, either, what with so many people being at the preaching. Someone might think it would be a good time to try a little breaking and entering. He'd stroll by the whorehouses, too, just to make sure the customers weren't playing too rough. He might not have wanted the sheriff's job, but as long as he had it, he was going to take it seriously.

He figured the Reverend Davis's service would go on for another couple of hours, more or less. By that time, Mitch would have finished checking out the town, and he could walk back down by the tent to make sure there weren't any incidents as a result of the preacher's enthusiastic condemnation of one of the town's more popular sins. You never knew what might get a fight started in a town like Paxton.

Mitch remembered something he'd heard someone say about a sermon once: "That preacher's stopped preachin' and started meddlin'." Mitch smiled, something he didn't do often. Davis hadn't waited long to begin his meddling, not long at all.

Chapter Three

The woman who called herself by the single name of Star was really Elizabeth Miller. She'd had a husband once, but that had been a few years back. He hadn't been much of a man, and when he'd gotten himself killed in a bar fight, Elizabeth hadn't really mourned, at least not about his death. She'd mourned more for her own situation, since the no-good skunk had died without leaving her a thing other than his oppressive debts.

She quickly found out that there wasn't much way for a woman alone to make money, certainly not enough money to pay what her dead husband had owed. So instead of paying, she left town.

That didn't solve her problems, but it helped her avoid them for a short while. When she found herself broke in a strange town, she thought of several jobs that she might try, but she had no education and very little ambition. That was when she looked at herself in a mirror, decided that she didn't look too bad for a woman her age, and figured that she had at least one skill that she could sell.

It turned out that she was right, and she became one of the more popular ladies at a sporting house in Denver. But after a year or two her looks began to decline, and only the less choosy or more drunken customers had any interest in her. So she moved on.

She discovered that in boomtowns, where women of any kind were in short supply and where the respectable ones were untouchable, a sporting lady's looks weren't nearly as important as her willingness. And that was how she wound up in Paxton.

She'd had a long, hard night at Fanny Belle's, because several of the ladies had taken the night off to see what the new preacher in town had to say. That gave Star more customers than usual, which she didn't mind at all. She tried to show them all a good time, even the ones who could have used a good bath, which was most of them. She didn't really mind that, either. There had been a time when it might have bothered her, but that was years ago.

She slipped out the back of Fanny Belle's tent sometime well after midnight. There was no one else around, but that didn't bother Star. She liked having a little time alone. She was going to walk the quarter mile to the house, really nothing more than a hastily thrown-together shack, where she was living with three other women who worked for Fanny Belle. Two of them had already left, and one, who called herself Rainbow, was servicing her last customer of the night.

Rainbow had been to the preaching, and she'd told Star a little about it.

"That preacher was really down on us whores," Rainbow said. "He said we were the spawn of the devil and on the road to hell. He really worked that crowd up, too. I'll bet half of them were ready to tar and feather us."

"And half of that half was probably here last night for a little poke," Star said.

Rainbow laughed. "You know it. Maybe more of them than that were here. But tonight they were feeling really righteous."

Star wasn't worried about being run out of town. She didn't think there was any danger of it happening. She and her sisters in sin provided a service that was too highly valued by too many of the citizens of Paxton.

She walked along the alley and was nearly to the street when she heard a slurred voice from the shadows.

"Hey, girlie. How 'bout a little fun?"

Star was tired, but she was game. She never turned down an honest dollar, and this would be one she wouldn't have to share with Fanny Belle. So she walked over to where a dark figure leaned against the wall of a saloon that fronted on the street.

"What're you looking for?" she asked.

"Just a little fun, like I said."

"You have money?"

"Sure do."

Star wasn't stupid. "Let's see it."

A hand reached into a pocket and came out with a coin.

"I can't see it," Star said.

"Then come over here."

Star walked over into the shadows and said, "Hand it to me."

"Not till I see what you've got, girlie. Pull up that dress and give us a look."

Star had long ago lost any sense of modesty that she might have had. She gave no more thought to pulling up her dress than she would have to swatting a fly.

"Not bad, girlie. Now give us a little kiss."

Star leaned forward. The knife was so sharp that she hardly felt it when it went into her stomach and began to tear the life out of her.

Chapter Four

Mitch was eating breakfast early the next morning when Jim Tyler came running into the Eat Here. He looked around the place for Mitch, and when he saw him, he ran over to where the sheriff was sitting.

He paused to catch his breath, and then he said, "Come quick, Sheriff. There's something you gotta see."

Mitch looked down at his half-eaten eggs and bacon. It seemed like nearly every time he sat down to eat lately, someone interrupted him.

"What's the trouble?" he asked.

Tyler looked around again. "I don't want to say right here. You better come on with me right now, though."

Mitch stood up. "All right. But this had better be important."

"It is," Tyler said. His hands were shaking like he was freezing cold. "You can bet on that."

Mitch followed Tyler outside. Tyler was a little man with bushy hair that he kept stuck under a squashed-looking hat, a bristly salt-and-pepper beard, and bandy legs. He had a mine up the mountain that he called the Elbow Grease, and Mitch had spoken to him casually a time or two in the past.

When they were outside the tent, Mitch said, "All right, Tyler, now you can talk. Tell me what's going on."

"You need to see it for yourself, Sheriff. Come on."

Responding to the urgency in Tyler's voice, Mitch followed him down the street. When they got to an alley near the Bad Dog Saloon, Tyler turned in.

"It was a dog that let me in on it," Tyler said. "It come out of the alley with what looked like somebody's hand in its mouth. I took me a look, and by God, it *was* somebody's hand."

Mitch wasn't sure he'd heard right. "Somebody's hand? Where is it now?"

"Damned if I know. That damned dog took off with it. Run under the porch of the saloon there. Prob'ly under there chewin' on it right now, for all I know."

"Where did a hand come from?" Mitch asked.

"That's the bad part," Tyler said, stopping at a gap between the saloon and the hotel it backed up to. "Look here, Sheriff."

Mitch looked.

He was a hard man, a man who'd thought very little at one time of cutting off the heads of men he'd killed, filling the heads with sand, and turning in the heads for the bounty he was due.

He'd ridden after Geronimo with Al Sieber and Tom Horn, and he'd seen what the Apaches could do to someone they had a particular hate for.

But he'd never seen anything quite like the sight in the alley that morning. Someone had cut a woman to pieces. There was blood mixed in with the dirt of the alley and soaking into the woman's clothing. Her hands had been cut off, and her stomach had been torn open to expose her innards. Her face had been hacked so badly that she was unrecognizable.

Flies were buzzing around, and Mitch was glad he hadn't finished that breakfast.

"What're you gonna do, Sheriff?" Tyler asked, his eyes wide.

"Damned if I know," Mitch said.

Evan Riley had red hair, freckles, and a wide grin most of the time. He ran the lumber yard in Paxton. He was also the town's coffin maker and undertaker. He wasn't grinning when he talked to Mitch about the body from the alley.

"Worst thing I ever saw," he said. "By a damn sight. How about you, Doc?"

Doc Feyden was short and bald, and he sported white sidewhiskers. He wore spectacles that always looked as if they were about to slide off the end of his nose, which they sometimes did when he was drunk. He was drunk just about every night, but he was the only thing resembling a doctor in Paxton.

"Didn't show a great deal of medical skill," Doc said. "Just butchery, that's all."

"I got her in the box," Riley said. "Most of her. But there's parts of her ain't there."

"Which parts?" Mitch asked.

"There's a hand missing, for one thing."

"Dog got it," Mitch said. "That's how Jim Tyler found the body."

"Oh. Well, there's an ear missing, too. You reckon the dog got that?"

Mitch said he didn't know.

"Could've been a cat," Riley said. "Ears are pretty small." He paused for a second. "The other one was still on her head. Wonder why he didn't cut 'em both off?"

"Who's he?" Mitch asked.

"The killer, that's who."

"Could've been a woman," Mitch said.

Riley shook his head in disagreement. Doc Feyden said, "I don't think a woman would kill somebody this way. This is a man's work. You can trust my judgment as a medical man on that."

Mitch wasn't sure how much of a medical man Feyden really was. It didn't seem likely that Feyden had ever actually studied medicine in a school, or at least not for very long. That would have required that he remain sober. But Mitch thought he might be right about the killer.

"Why would someone do a thing like that?" Mitch asked. "In your judgment as a medical man."

Doc pushed his glasses up on his nose. "Have to be crazy. No other explanation. A normal man wouldn't do it. A normal man might kill somebody because he was jealous or mad or for some other reason. But he'd have a reason, and he'd just make a clean kill. He wouldn't butcher a person."

"So you think we've got a crazy man living here in Paxton," Mitch said.

"Either that, or he's already left."

"Let's hope he's left, then."

"I wouldn't bet on it," Riley said.

"Me, neither," said Doc.

Mitch didn't say anything. He was wondering how he was supposed to go about finding a crazy man.

"There's something else," Riley said, breaking into Mitch's thoughts.

"What's that?"

"That woman in the box. We don't know who she is. How you gonna find that out?"

"That should be the easy part," Mitch said.

In fact, Mitch already had a pretty good general idea of the dead woman's identity. If she'd been one of the few respectable women in town, he'd have already heard about it. Which meant that she was one of the others.

He walked back through town by way of a couple of the whorehouses, including Fanny Belle's, which was closest to where the body had been found. Fanny Belle was the only one there at that hour of the morning, and she'd obviously awakened not long before. Her hair was down, and her large body was wrapped in some kind of red dressing gown that had seen better days.

"Come in the tent, Sheriff," she said when she saw Mitch at the entrance. "It's a little early for sportin', but I'll see if I can find you somebody who's interested."

The place was set up with cots separated from one another and from the open area in front by sheets hung on ropes. It smelled of sweat and whiskey and sour linen.

"I didn't come here for sportin'," Mitch said. "I came here to ask if any of your girls had turned up missing."

Fanny Belle took a drink from the dirty glass she was holding. Mitch figured he knew where the whiskey smell was coming from.

"I wouldn't know about that," she said when she'd had her sip. "A couple of 'em went to hear that preacher last night and didn't come in for work. Maybe he converted 'em."

"The one I'm talking about didn't look converted," Mitch said, and he told her about the woman that had been found in the alley.

"Jesus, Mary, and Joseph," Fanny Belle said when he was finished, and she drained her glass. "You shouldn't tell a woman stories like that so early in the day."

Mitch didn't bother to point out that it wasn't early in the day at all, not for someone who kept more or less normal hours. He said, "I need to know who she was. Then I'll have to ask you about who she saw last night."

"I don't keep up with who the girls see. Long as I get my money, that's all I care about. And as for who she was, I don't know that either. I don't keep up with the girls after they've left here."

"Where do they go when they leave?" Mitch asked, and Fanny Belle told him.

Mitch didn't have anything against whores. He'd associated with them for a good part of his life, and now and then he'd conducted a business transaction with one, usually when he'd had more to drink than was good for him. He'd never called on one socially before, though he supposed that what he was doing now didn't really qualify as a social call. It was more like business, but not the kind of business that he liked.

The girls didn't like it either.

"Why should we tell you anything?" asked the one called Rainbow. "Are you trying to make trouble for us?"

Mitch looked around the shack. The women who lived there didn't do much to keep it up. It hadn't been cleaned in several weeks, if ever. There was a smell of garbage in the air, and under that the smell of whiskey.

"I'm not trying to make trouble for anybody," he said. "Somebody's already made the trouble. I'm just trying to find out who it was made for."

"What's that supposed to mean?" a redhead asked.

She wasn't a natural redhead, and she wasn't wearing much more than a chemise. Her lack of clothing didn't affect Mitch, who found her a little skinny for his tastes. Besides, she had bad teeth.

"It means somebody killed a woman last night in the alley behind Fanny Belle's place," Mitch said. "I'm trying to find out who she was."

The women looked at one another. "Why would you care?" the redhead asked.

"Because it's my job. And it might help me find out who killed her."

"What does it matter to you? She was just a whore." The redhead's mouth twisted. "Like the rest of us."

"It don't matter what she was. I'm the sheriff, and I'm going to find out who killed her and see that the law has its way with him."

"What a load of crap," the third woman said.

She had black hair, as black as any hair Mitch had ever seen, even among the Apache. He figured she probably put something on it to make it that color.

"It's not crap," Mitch said. "I have a job to do, and I'll do it."

He was telling the truth, which surprised him just a little. He might not have asked for the job, but now that he had it, he was going to do it the best he could. He didn't know why he cared enough to feel that way, but there was no denying that he did.

The redhead looked him in the eye. "Maybe

you will, at that. All right, I'll tell you who it might be. She was staying here with us. She said her name was Star, but nobody goes by their real name. I'm called Rose." She pointed to the brunette. That's Carmen, and the skinny one's Rainbow. We haven't seen Star since last night."

"She was at Fanny Belle's last night, though," Rainbow said. "I talked to her there after I got back from the preaching. Do you think she's the one that was killed?"

Mitch nodded. "Seems like a good possibility."

At least he'd gotten one piece of information. If Star was indeed the dead woman, he knew that she hadn't been killed until after the Reverend Davis's services had broken up."

"What can you tell me about her?"

"We just told you all we know."

"How old was she? What color hair did she have?"

"She was a little older than we are," Carmen said. "Her hair was brown."

The way the dead woman had been cut up, there wasn't any way for Mitch to estimate her age. But she'd had brown hair. So did a lot of women, but he suspected that Star was the murdered woman.

"What about her real name?" he asked.

"Elizabeth, I think," Rose said. "But don't ask me her last name. I don't know it."

The other two didn't either. They might have talked among themselves about some things, maybe even about their pasts, but there were some things that remained forever unsaid.

"Any special customers?" Mitch asked. "People who always asked for her?"

They were no more helpful on that point than

39

Fanny Belle had been, and Mitch told them that if they thought of anything that might help, they should be sure to get in touch with him. But he didn't really think they would.

On his way back to his office, Mitch stopped off in the alley behind Fanny Belle's. He wanted to have another look at the place where Tyler had found the body, not that he thought there'd be anything helpful there. He'd given the spot a pretty good going-over the first time and hadn't located anything that might lead him to a killer.

There had been blood, but Mitch figured that had all come from Star (he was already thinking of the dead woman by that name), and it wouldn't have mattered if it hadn't. He couldn't tell one person's blood from another's.

He'd looked around for boot tracks, but he hadn't found anything useful. That was a shame, since in his first days on the job, a boot track had helped him nail a killer. But it hadn't rained for quite a while, and the dirt in the alley was as hard as an oak board.

He inspected the boards on the sides of the buildings, hoping he might find a piece of cloth snagged on a splinter or a nail, but there was nothing.

He got down on his knees and looked under the buildings. Maybe the killer had dropped something. If Mitch was lucky, maybe even the killer's knife was under there.

Mitch wasn't lucky. He could see nothing at all.

While he was on his knees, a scruffy-looking dog came nosing along, sniffing at the blood. It wasn't the same dog that had run off with the hand, which Mitch had retrieved earlier.

"Clear from here, dog," Mitch said. "There's nothing for you."

There was nothing for Mitch, either. He stood up and dusted off his pants.

The dog looked up at him expectantly.

"Forget it, dog," Mitch said, and headed to his office.

Chapter Five

When Mitch got back to his office, Jewel Reid was sitting behind his desk.

"Your father sits there when he comes in, too," Mitch said. "Doesn't anybody know who the sheriff is around here?"

Jewel smiled at him. "I know, all right. But there's something I don't know."

"What?"

"I don't know who was killed last night."

Mitch sat in the room's other chair and leaned it back so that it was resting on its two back legs.

"I guess the word's got around," he said.

"Oh, yes. People aren't talking about much else."

Mitch had known the murder would make talk. It wasn't so much the murder that people were interested in; it was the gruesomeness of it.

"Did you happen to hear who did it?" he asked.

"Of course," Jewel said. "The new preacher did it."

The front legs of Mitch's chair hit the floor with a thud. "Then I'd better go down to arrest him."

Jewel laughed. "You don't really believe he did it, do you? He's a preacher, after all."

"You ever had much dealings with preachers?"

"Not much."

"Then you don't know them. But let me tell you, no matter what they'd like you to think, they're no different from anybody else. And that Deuce Davis don't like scarlet women. That much is plain enough."

"So that's who was killed. What was her name?"

"She called herself Star, but her name was Elizabeth. Don't know the last name. She never told anybody."

"Is that going to make it harder to find her killer?"

Jewel was getting interested, which was no surprise to Mitch. He had to admit that she'd been a big help when he was trying to figure out who'd bashed those miners' heads in. In fact, she'd had a couple of mighty good ideas. She might be able to help him out this time, too.

There was one drawback to that plan, however, and Mitch was well aware of it. While there was no question of Jewel's eagerness to help or of her ability, her father didn't approve of her associating with Mitch. It didn't make any difference that Mitch was the sheriff—and the sheriff of J. Paxton Reid's own choosing, to boot. Mitch was still half Apache, and Reid couldn't get past that. When you got right down to it, he thought his daughter was too good for the likes of Mitch Frye.

But Reid wasn't around at the moment, and Jewel didn't seem to have the same kind of feelings that her father did, anyway. So Mitch decided to see what Jewel thought about things.

"I'm not sure that we have to know her name," he said. "If you don't think the preacher did it, who do you think did?"

Jewel put her elbows on the desk and leaned forward. Mitch liked the line of her body, the gleam of excitement in her eyes, the way her clean, shiny hair caught the light. After Fanny Belle's women, Jewel was like a breath of mountain air. *You ought not to be thinking that way, boy*, Mitch told himself.

"It could be that the preacher did it," Jewel said. "Indirectly."

"You didn't see her," Mitch said. "She was killed about as directly as anybody could be."

"That's not what I meant. What if there was someone at the preaching last night who took the preacher's meaning a little too much to heart?"

Mitch saw what she was getting at. "You mean someone decided God had talked to him and told him to clean up this town, get rid of all the scarlet women."

"Scarlet women? That's the second time you've used that expression. You can say *whores* in front of me."

Mitch felt the tips of his ears getting red. Any other woman he'd ever known, he'd have said *whores* without thinking about it. He didn't understand what there was about Jewel that made him feel different when he was around her.

It was a scary thought. And even scarier was the thought that maybe he *did* know why he felt different around her.

He shook off those reflections and got back to the topic at hand. "Let's don't worry about my language. Let's talk about your idea. Who did you see there last night that might get off the rails like that, just because of what a preacher said?"

"That would be hard to figure. It could have been anyone."

"Your father was there."

"You didn't have to say that."

"It makes sense," Mitch told her. "Paxton's his town. He's the mayor, and he put his brand on it. Stands to reason that he'd want it to be a place where families might come someday and put down their roots. Make it a permanent settlement."

"He wouldn't be stupid enough to think he could change the town by killing one whore at a time."

"Kill one, scare off the rest."

"Not likely. Did you hear of any of them leaving town today?"

Mitch admitted that he hadn't. He tried to remember who he'd seen at the services.

"Did you see anyone getting particularly worked up?" he asked.

"Plenty," Jewel said. "You left before the preacher got wound up. It was a rip-roaring sermon by the time he was finished."

"He was going pretty good while I was there," Mitch said.

"It got better. Or worse, depending on how you look at it."

"Well, it might not matter. There's plenty of other reasons why somebody might want to kill a . . . a whore."

Jewel grinned. "Now, that wasn't so bad, was it? What other reasons would there be?"

"She might've robbed somebody. They do that sometimes. Or she might've given somebody a disease. Or maybe somebody was just drunk and did something last night that he doesn't even remember doing this morning."

"You don't really believe that last one, do you?"

"You never can tell," Mitch said.

"I can tell you one thing, though," Jewel said.

"What's that?"

"There's going to be another sermon tonight."

"And you think that might cause more trouble?"

"I don't know," Jewel said. "But then, I'm not the sheriff. Have you eaten lunch?"

Mitch said that he hadn't.

"Then why don't we do that?"

Mitch shrugged. It sounded like a fine idea to him.

After a lunch of what Ellie West swore was venison stew and cornbread, Mitch spent the afternoon talking to as many of the town's whores as he could. None of them could tell him anything new about Star, and none of them seemed very worried about being killed. They seemed to think that if anyone was to blame for Star's death, it was Star.

"She was just careless, is all," one of the women told Mitch. "There are plenty of men that like to get rough. You have to know how to handle them, and you have to be careful. She wasn't."

Mitch didn't think it was as simple as that, though he couldn't have explained why. It was just a feeling. He went back to Fanny Belle's to talk to the madam.

"Sure, there are men who like it rough," she said.

She smelled even more strongly of whiskey than she had that morning. Mitch wondered how much she drank in a day. Well, it wasn't any of his business, as long as she didn't cause any trouble in the town.

"How rough?" he asked.

"As rough as you'll let 'em get. But they're not gonna do that in any house I run. I don't allow it, and I tell all my girls not to allow it."

"You think Star maybe forgot what you told her?"

"Star knew better than to forget. Besides, she wasn't killed in here. She was killed outside."

There was no sentimentality in Fanny Belle's voice, and Mitch was sure she hadn't shed a tear for Star. If anything, she sounded a little angry. Fanny Belle didn't care much about people. She just wanted her share of the money they made, and now she was short one worker.

"Just the same, you might let all your girls know what happened."

"Don't you worry about my girls," Fanny Belle said. "They can all take care of themselves."

Just like Star did, Mitch thought. He said, "I hope you're right."

"I'm right, Sheriff. Don't worry about me."

Mitch decided that he wouldn't.

The sermon that night was even more inflammatory than the first one had been. Davis stalked up and down behind the pulpit, waving his Bible and calling for hellfire to consume any man who mingled with harlots and saying that Star's death was the just judgment of God, who had reached out his omnipotent hand and struck her down for her sins.

Mitch couldn't listen to much of it. He'd met more than enough people in his life who hated him for what he was, and he wasn't going to spend a minute more than he had to listening to someone preach hate against another person. He didn't think it was right, and he didn't have the stomach to listen to it.

He did take the time to look over the congregation to see if anyone was getting unduly excited. If anyone was, he couldn't tell. There was plenty of head nodding, and a number of people were shouting "Amen!" to some of the preacher's more vehement remarks, but no one stood out in Mitch's mind.

He was interested to see that J. Paxton Reid was there again, and for that matter so was everyone else Mitch had noticed the previous evening. In fact, the crowd was somewhat larger, as if the preacher had a greater appeal than Mitch would have guessed. People seemed eager to hear his condemnations. Mitch supposed that shouldn't have been surprising.

The surprising thing was the presence of Tolliver and Spivey, who were right back near the front of the tent, even though this time Mitch wasn't coercing them. Maybe they were getting religion.

Before Mitch slipped away, he asked Jewel to keep an eye out for anything unusual, and she said she would. When Mitch left the tent, Reid glared at him. Mitch touched the brim of his hat politely in return.

The town was quiet when Mitch made his rounds. With so many people at the preacher's tent, there were fewer customers at the whorehouses, and there were fewer gamblers and drinkers at the saloons. Mitch figured that there were some people who'd be just as glad to have the Reverend Deuce Davis pack up his tent and move on out of town.

Red Collins, the owner of the Bad Dog Saloon, was one man who'd be glad. He had red hair, and his face was always flushed. He'd been a gambler at one time, but he'd been smarter than most and had known when to quit. He'd saved his money, too, unlike most gamblers, and invested it in the Bad Dog.

"That son of a bitch is going to put me out of business," Red told Mitch.

"Don't look that way to me," Mitch said, looking out across the room.

The poker tables weren't full, but there were

gamblers at all of them. The roulette wheel was spinning, and the faro game was going strong.

"There's about half the usual crowd," Collins said. "I tell you, I wish that preacher would find some other town to save from its sins."

"I don't think he's saved this one yet," Mitch said.

"And he's not going to. I never knew of a town yet that got saved by any hellfire preacher, or by anybody else in that line of work." Collins looked at Mitch. "Unless maybe it was by an honest sheriff."

"Us honest sheriffs don't mind a preacher who can keep a town as quiet as this one is," Mitch said. "I haven't had to break up a fight or stop a shooting or even put anybody in jail since Deuce Davis got to town."

"You had to bury somebody, though," Collins pointed out.

"Yeah, that's a real drawback, all right."

"Besides," Collins said, "I don't think Mr. Davis has been a preacher all his life."

"You know something about him?"

"I might. Used to be a gambler a few years back, stuck mostly to riverboats, and he was called Deuce because he just had two fingers on his left hand."

"That sounds like Davis all right, except he lost his fingers to a grizzly bear up on the Yellowstone."

"Who told you that? Davis?"

"He didn't tell me. He told somebody else. But I see your point. You ever sit across the table from that two-fingered gambler?"

"Once. You'd think he wouldn't be able to handle the cards with a hand like that, but he was as slick as anybody I ever saw."

Mitch glanced at Collins's hands. They were big

and blocky and looked too clumsy to handle cards, yet Mitch knew that Collins had been very successful at the tables.

Collins saw where Mitch was looking. "Yeah, a pair of hands can fool you. Anyway, this guy was good. I heard he had to leave the river after a while. Some fella caught him in bed with his wife and nearly killed him."

"How?"

"Sliced his face wide open with a Bowie knife, the way I heard it," Collins said.

That would explain the scar on Davis's face. Mitch said, "I wish you'd take a look at our preacher when you get a chance. Sounds like he's the man you met, all right. I don't see that we should hold that against him, though."

Collins looked out at the half-empty room. "I hold it against him that my business is down. I'll have a look at him. You reckon the services are still going on?"

"You can practically hear him from here."

"Then I'll walk on down and give him a gander. See you later, Sheriff."

"Yeah," Mitch said.

Chapter Six

Carrie Mae Winslow was younger than Star had been by ten years. She was chubby and pretty, and she had sparkling eyes. She had curly blond hair that she wore in ringlets that hung to her almost-always-bare shoulders, and she was by far the most popular of all the girls who worked the upstairs of the Bad Dog Saloon.

She was glad that she worked in the Bad Dog instead of some tent like Fanny Belle's. The customers were a little cleaner, and they spent a little more money for their pleasures. And there was considerably more privacy. Carrie Mae wasn't shy, but she didn't like to listen to the sounds other people made while she was earning her living.

Sooner or later, and more likely sooner if things followed their natural course, Carrie Mae would find her prettiness fading as the sparkle died from her eyes. Then she'd be looking for work in a place like Fanny Belle's. But that was something Carrie Mae never thought about, or, if she did, she pushed it right out of her head.

She had only one dangerous habit. Every night, or early morning, after she'd turned all her tricks, she liked to go outside and walk for a few minutes and smoke a hand-rolled cigarette. She could roll a smoke quicker than any man she'd ever met, and she was a little vain about her skill.

She liked the silence of the town in the hours of the very early morning when no one was around, when all the other girls who worked the Bad Dog were going to bed and all the men who'd been drinking and gambling and screwing had gone back to wherever it was that they lived. She liked it that no one ever bothered her.

Until that night. Just as she stepped off the boardwalk near O'Connor's Mercantile, someone called to her from the alley.

"Hey, girlie. How's about a little fun?"

She ignored the voice. She was through for the night, and she wasn't going to mess with some drunk in an alley. She didn't need the money. It had been a slow night at the Bad Dog, that was true enough, but there had been plenty of good nights before that. She took a puff of her hand-rolled smoke and kept right on walking.

A hand reached out of the darkness and gripped her wrist like a steel band.

"Let me go, you son of a bitch," Carrie Mae said, but she was pulled relentlessly into the alley.

She dropped her cigarette to the ground and opened her mouth to scream, but a large, powerful hand was clamped over it. She smelled sweat and bad breath.

"I thought you and me could have a good time, girlie. You don't need to put up a fight."

Carrie Mae tried to get a hand loose to scratch

the bastard's face, but she found that both her arms were held tight against her.

"It's all right if you fight a little, girlie. I like a woman that'll fight back."

Carrie Mae was damned if she was going to give the son of a bitch the satisfaction of doing anything he liked. She went limp in his arms.

"Well, well. I like it that way too, you know."

Carrie Mae didn't know, not that it mattered, for within seconds of the time the razor-sharp blade sliced through the soft skin of her throat, she knew nothing at all ever again.

Chapter Seven

There was a little room in back of the sheriff's office that served as Mitch's living quarters. He was awakened by the sound of someone pounding on the front door. He looked around and saw that it was early morning, the dark just beginning to turn to gray outside the window. He rolled into a sitting position, slipped on his jeans, and jammed his feet into his boots.

"I'm coming," he said as he walked into the office.

He opened the door and saw John O'Connor standing there. O'Connor had on a white storekeeper's apron, and sweat stood out in beads on the top of his bald head. He was shaking like a man with the palsy.

"You gotta come quick, Sheriff," he said. "There's a dead woman behind my store."

"Goddamn it," Mitch said. "You go get Doc Feyden and Evan Riley. I'll meet you at the store."

O'Connor didn't say anything. He turned to go.

"Just a minute," Mitch said.

O'Connor turned back.

"What did she look like?" Mitch asked.

"Like a butchered calf," O'Connor answered.

Mitch had thought that might be the case. "Go on, then. I'll be there as soon as I can."

The woman was cut up in the same amateur fashion that Star had been. Both hands had been removed, but this time no dogs had gotten to them. They lay in the dirt beside the body. The smell was pretty bad. Beside the offal, O'Connor had puked when he stumbled across the dead woman.

"Any idea who she was?" Mitch asked Doc Feyden.

"Not much left of her face," Feyden said.

His skin was an unhealthy gray color, and his eyes were red. He probably hadn't had much more sleep than Mitch, and he'd undoubtedly been drunk when he went to bed.

"I think I've seen that dress before," Mitch said, trying to place it. The last time he'd seen it, it hadn't been saturated with blood.

"One of the girls from the Bad Dog," Evan Riley said, joining them. "I know the dress."

"Better go wake up Red," Mitch said. "He needs to know about this."

Evan left them and went to get the saloon owner.

"Looks like it was done by the same person who killed the other one," Feyden said. "He's not very careful how he goes about it."

Mitch looked around for anything that might give him a hint as to the killer's identity. He didn't find a thing. No boot prints, nothing that anyone had dropped to the ground except for the stub of a hand-rolled cigarette. He didn't think that would be much help. Nearly everybody in Paxton rolled smokes.

Including Mitch, who took the makings from his pocket, rolled a cigarette, lit it, and took a deep puff. He was blowing out a white plume of smoke when Riley and Red Collins showed up.

"Sweet Jesus," Collins said. "That's Carrie Mae."

"Not anymore," Mitch said.

Later that morning, Mitch went to Star's burial. There was hardly anyone there except him and a couple of the whores from Fanny Belle's. Fanny Belle herself didn't bother to come. J. Paxton Reid was there, along with Jewel, but there was no preacher, so one of the whores asked Reid to say a few words. He recited a couple of Bible verses that Mitch didn't recognize. No surprise there, considering the depth of his acquaintanceship with the Bible.

When the grave digger began to cover the casket, Reid walked over to Mitch and said, "Do you think there was any connection between the murder of this girl and the one that was found this morning?"

"Don't you?" Mitch said.

"Of course there was," Jewel put in. "How could there be any question about it?"

Reid looked at her, then at Mitch. "What are you going to do?"

Mitch rolled a smoke, lit it, and said, "Whatever I can. I'll talk to that preacher first, see if I can get him to tone down his sermons, or maybe move on to another subject."

"You think he has anything to do with this?"

"Don't know. Could be that he's stirring someone up."

"It has to stop," Reid said. "I don't like this kind of thing happening in my town."

Mitch exhaled smoke. "I don't like it, either. I'll do what I can."

He turned and started away. Jewel walked along beside him.

"Your father isn't going to like it if you go with me," Mitch told her. He tossed his cigarette to the ground and crushed it under his boot heel.

Jewel looked back at Reid, who was staring after them with obvious animosity.

"I can't help that. I need to talk to you about last night's service."

"What about it?"

"I was watching out to see who really got excited by what Davis had to say. I have some names for you."

Mitch stopped and turned to her. "I don't want you to get mixed up in this. Whoever's doing the killing doesn't like women. I wouldn't want anything to happen to you."

"That's about the sweetest thing you've ever said to me. If you don't watch out, I'll start thinking that you might like me."

Mitch looked back. Reid was still standing there.

"I just don't like the idea of you being involved in anything dangerous."

"You'd feel the same way about anyone?"

Mitch didn't answer.

"Anyway," Jewel said, "I noticed a few people who seemed very excited by the whole thing. One of them was John O'Connor."

Mitch found that very interesting. Both women had been killed near O'Connor's place of business.

"Who else?" he asked.

"George Kelley, for one."

Mitch found it hard to think of the banker as a killer, but he knew better than to discount anyone.

"Any others?"

Jewel hesitated. Then she said, "Bill Carson."

"Your father's manager. You know him pretty well, don't you?"

"I know him. I'm not sure how well."

"Who else?"

"I don't know that this is worth mentioning, but Ellie West seemed really intense."

Mitch hadn't entirely given up the idea that a woman could be the killer, though it seemed unlikely, as Doc Feyden had pointed out. And Ellie West was a big, strong woman.

"Is that it?"

"There were plenty of others who seemed to agree with what Davis had to say, but not as much as those."

"What about your father?"

"I don't know why you keep on bringing him into it."

"He has a reason."

"Let me tell you something about my father. He knows that whores are a necessary part of a boomtown. Can you imagine what this place would be like if they weren't here?"

Mitch thought about it. "There would be a lot more fighting and shooting, I expect. And maybe the few respectable women in town would be in a little more danger than they already are."

"Of course. You wouldn't want to be the sheriff of a place like that."

Mitch started to say that he didn't want to be the sheriff of any place at all, but for the first time since Paxton had tricked him into taking the job, he realized that he actually sort of liked what he was doing. People in Paxton respected him, and most of them seemed to think he was doing a good job. For the first time in his life, it was as if he belonged somewhere. For a man who'd spent most of his life living on the edges of society and always on the move, it was an odd feeling. And a pretty good one.

He wondered how people would feel about him if he found out that one of their respected citizens was a killer.

He wondered how he would feel.

He managed to get rid of Jewel by asking if she shouldn't be at work. He didn't want her with him when he paid a visit to Evan Riley.

Riley had the casket made and the body inside when Mitch arrived. He didn't look as if he felt very well.

"This was worse than the first one," he told Mitch.

"Worse how?"

"I don't know. Maybe it wasn't worse. Maybe it was just that she was the second one. I'm thinking of getting out of the casket business."

"Was she all there?" Mitch asked.

"Funny you should ask that."

"Why?"

"She was missing an ear."

Mitch went back to his office to think. Writing things down seemed to help him organize his thoughts, so he sat at his desk and sharpened a pencil with his penknife. He started writing on the back of a wanted dodger that had recently come in:

1. Women being killed—whores.
2. Ears missing—killer keeping them?
3. Women butchered—killer must really hate women or whores.
4. Preacher stirring up town against whores—coincidence?

   5. George Kelley, Bill Carson, John O'Connor,
      Ellie West.
   6. The Reverend Deuce Davis.

He looked over the list, folded it, and put it in the
desk drawer. He decided to start at the bottom.

Davis was staying in the Palace Hotel. Mitch went
there after a little side trip to the Bad Dog Saloon.
Mitch had never seen a real palace, but he suspected that if he ever did, it wouldn't look a thing
like the Palace Hotel. The desk clerk said that
Davis was in room 12.

   "He been out this morning?" Mitch asked.

   "Went out for breakfast. He's been back for a
good while."

   Mitch went to the room and knocked on the
door.

   "Who's there?"

   "Mitch Frye. I'm the sheriff here in Paxton."

   Davis came to the door and opened it a crack.
He looked out at Mitch. "What do you want?"

   "I have to talk to you. We can do it here, or you
can come over to my office."

   Davis pulled the door open. "Come on in."

   The preacher was wearing his black suit, and
he did in fact look a lot like a gambler. Mitch had
met a few of those in his day, and many of them
liked to wear black broadcloth suits, white shirts,
and black ties. Maybe they thought a suit made a
man respectable.

   The room had a bed, a washstand with a basin
sitting on it, and one chair. Mitch walked over
and sat in the chair. Davis remained standing.

   "What's the trouble, Sheriff?"

   "I expect you've heard."

   Davis walked over to the room's only window

and stood looking out with his hands clasped behind his back.

"If it's about those women who've been killed, I had nothing to do with it."

Mitch looked at the preacher's hands. "Must've been hard, learning to deal seconds with those fingers missing."

Davis turned to face him, concealing his hands. "I'm afraid I don't know what you're talking about, Sheriff. What does 'dealing seconds' mean?"

"Come on, Davis. Give it up. I just went by and talked to Red Collins, who knows you from the old days. You used to be a riverboat gambler until somebody took a dislike to you and cut you up a little."

Davis's good hand went to the scar on his face, touched it lightly, then dropped down to his side.

"Red Collins. I thought I saw him in the crowd last night. He was quite a gambler in his day. I sat in on a hand or two with him years back."

"So you admit that you're a gambler."

"*Was* a gambler, Sheriff. I haven't touched a deck of cards in years, not since I saw the error of my ways. Gambling leads a man to drinking, and drinking leads him to other things. Worse things."

"Like sleeping with other men's wives."

"That woman was no better than a harlot. She'd slept with half the men on that riverboat." Davis's hand went to the scar again. "It was just my bad luck to be the one that got caught."

"Thing like that might make a man dislike women quite a bit."

"I can see where you're headed, Sheriff, but you're wrong about me. Since I was saved by the Lord, I've led a very quiet life. I haven't had a

61

drink in years, or touched a deck of cards. And I certainly haven't touched a woman, not to love her or to kill her."

"You preach against women pretty strong, though."

"Not women. Just a certain kind of woman, the kind of woman that can take a man straight to hell and leave him to burn in the everlasting fire."

Davis's voice began to rise, and his eyes took on a fanatical gleam.

"I didn't come here for a sermon," Mitch said. "Mainly I came to ask you what you did after your services last night. And the night before."

"I came here to my room. I read my Bible, I prayed, and I went to bed."

"That's it?"

"That's it. I didn't kill anyone, Sheriff."

"You carry a gun, Davis?"

"I never liked guns. Not even when I wasn't a preacher."

"What about knives?"

"I like knives even less than guns."

Mitch stood up. "You make a pretty good living, preaching those hellfire sermons of yours?"

"I get by," Davis said. "People are often more generous in their giving than you might expect."

"And would it bother you if somebody who was giving you that offering took your words a little too seriously and went out to get rid of a few harlots so the world would be a better place?"

Davis thought for a second. "No, I don't suppose it would."

"And it doesn't bother you that all the time you're up there preaching the word, you're the same man that slept with somebody else's wife and got your face sliced open for it? Seems to me that's a little hypocritical."

"You can think what you want to," Davis said. "I admit that I'm a flawed human being.

That doesn't make my message any less true."

"You could be right," Mitch said. "I'll be seeing you."

"At the services tonight?"

"Maybe," Mitch said.

But he saw Davis before then, when somebody tried to burn the preacher's tent to the ground.

Chapter Eight

If there was one thing that everyone in Paxton feared, it was fire. Water was a scarce commodity up on the side of a mountain. There was a small, spring-fed stream that ran down the side of the mountain not far from town, and most of Paxton's water supply came from the stream. There wasn't a lot of water at the best of times, and there certainly wasn't enough to fight a large fire.

There was also no organized fire-fighting group in Paxton, so the flames that were roaring in the canvas of Davis's tent were big trouble. If the fire spread to any of the nearby tents or buildings, it could eventually consume the entire town.

Mitch found out about the fire when he heard people running and yelling in the street in front of his office. When he stepped out and saw the smoke, he joined the group that was running toward the fire.

By the time Mitch reached the tent, a bucket brigade had been formed. Men were lined up from the tent to the creek, with buckets of water being passed along and then tossed on the flames. It wasn't doing much good.

Mitch saw the Reverend Davis at the front of the line, but he wasn't doing anything to help. He was staring in consternation as the fire consumed his tent. The scar on his face stood out in livid relief on his fire-reddened countenance.

"Faster!" he screamed. "More water! We need more water!"

Mitch wondered why Davis wasn't hauling a bucket himself if he was so concerned. The flames were being fanned by the evening breeze, and bits of burning tent canvas were beginning to fly up into the air and float along toward town.

J. Paxton Reid appeared at Mitch's elbow.

"We have to stop it," he said. "What are you going to do?"

Mitch started to say that he hadn't been hired to fight fires, but Reid would probably have told him that fire fighting was part of the sheriff's job.

So he said, "Strike the tent."

"What?"

"Get the damned tent down," Mitch said, and started to yell orders to the men with the buckets.

At first it seemed that no one heard him, or maybe it was just that they couldn't believe what they were hearing. They ignored him and kept on with their buckets.

But Davis caught on.

"Cut the ropes, you hard-rock sons of bitches!" he yelled. "Get it down on the ground!"

He pulled a Bowie knife from his right boot and began slashing at the ropes that were tied to the tent pegs. Several others who had knives joined him, George Kelley, Sam Spivey, and Red

Collins among them. It was good to see someone like Spivey joining in with the town's solid citizens in a community effort. Maybe his time in jail had done him some good, Mitch thought. Or maybe it was his attention to Davis's sermons.

It didn't take long to collapse the tent, and then the men swarmed over it, trampling the flames and pouring buckets of water on them. Black smoke billowed up and choked them, but it was much easier to fight the fire without the tent billowing in the wind, and the sparks were kept to a minimum. It wasn't too long before the greatest danger had passed.

When things were under control, Reid, who had gotten his boots singed, looked consideringly at Mitch and said, "You're not as dumb as you look."

"I know you didn't hire me for my brains," Mitch told him. "But I can use them when I have to."

"Did you hear what Davis yelled a while ago?" Reid asked. "Pretty strong language for a preacher, if you ask me."

Mitch rubbed at a soot-stained cheek. "He wasn't always a preacher. Besides, you never know what somebody will say when he's excited."

"You think anybody else noticed?"

"Probably not, and nobody cared if they did."

Reid brushed ash off his jacket. "I wonder how the fire got started."

Mitch didn't have an answer for that one, but he saw Herman Tolliver talking to Davis, who was waving his arms in agitation. Before Mitch could walk over to see what was going on, Davis began to shout.

"It was the harlots!" he said. "It was the women scarlet with sin who feared the message that I bring to the town of Paxton, and they tried to burn me out. But they're the ones that will burn with the everlasting fires of hell, them and the men who lie with them!"

"Who was it, Preacher?" one of the firefighters yelled. "Who was it that set your tent on fire?"

"It was the harlot named Fanny Belle," Davis said. "She runs a house for fallen women, yet none have fallen so far as she has! God will punish her for her sins!"

"Why wait for God to do it?" someone yelled. "We can punish the hell out of her right now!"

"Damn right we can," came another yell. "Let's show those whores they can't mess around with God's house."

Mitch didn't think Davis would speak out and say anything about forgiveness; Davis's religion didn't seem big on forgiving. Mitch did think, though, that Davis might say a few words about how punishment was something best left up to God and that they should let divine justice prevail.

He didn't say anything of the kind, however. He said, "Who'll follow me to put the harlots to rout?"

Every man there except for Mitch, Reid, and a couple of others made some kind of positive response, and the next thing Mitch knew the whole crowd was marching up the street—a mob of men who not more than an hour before had been united in a good purpose, now equally determined on destruction.

"You have to stop them," Reid said.

"I agree," said Red Collins, who was standing beside them by this time. "I'd hate to think what a bunch like that could do to my saloon."

"I don't think they're going for your saloon," Mitch told him. "I think they're headed for Fanny Belle's."

"First her place, next mine. What can we do?"

Mitch didn't really know. He'd never dealt with

a mob before. He pulled his pistol and fired a couple of shots into the air.

A few of the men looked back. The others were so absorbed in their self-righteousness that they didn't even notice, and the ones who did notice didn't care. They turned back around and moved on up the street.

"Well, that was effective," Collins said dryly. "Why don't you throw a rock at them next. Maybe that'll get their attention."

Mitch didn't say anything. He started running for the jail. The men in the mob were shouldering along in the middle of the street, bumping each other, yelling insults, and stepping on one another's heels. Mitch had the advantage of being able to skirt around them, and before they'd gone too far, he was ahead of them. He reached his office, went inside, and got the shotgun he'd had Reid buy for him as part of the sheriff's defenses. In his experience, men who wouldn't blink at a pistol would think twice when they saw someone standing in front of them with a double-barrel.

He reached Fanny Belle's about thirty seconds before the mob, and he was able to take up his place in front of the tent and plant his feet.

Davis was leading the crowd, and he stopped short when he saw Mitch and the shotgun. He was obviously a man with a healthy respect for buckshot. A couple of the men behind him were less observant, and they bumped into him. Then they saw Mitch and stopped as well. It didn't take long for the whole sorry swarm to come to a halt. They all stood there muttering and cursing Mitch.

"Let's rush him. The son of a bitch can't get us all."

"Protecting whores! Is that what a sheriff's for? Reid will fire his ass as soon as he finds this out."

"Bet he's looking to get a piece of Fanny Belle for this!"

While they grumbled, Mitch didn't take his eyes off Davis. He waited until they'd had their say, or most of it, and then he spoke.

"Well, Preacher, are you going to call them off, or do you want me to shorten you by a foot or so? I could take your legs off at the knee before anybody could get to me."

Someone cried out, "Threatening a preacher now. The bastard!"

"What about it, Davis?" Mitch said, ignoring the voice from the mob. "Why don't you send them home."

Davis looked at him with eyes that burned with a fanaticism almost as hot as the fire that had destroyed his tent.

Red Collins and J. Paxton Reid bypassed the crowd and stepped up beside Mitch. Collins looked out over the heads of the men and said, "I know most of you fellas. A lot of you are customers of mine. You don't want to be hurting anybody or doing any harm to this place of business behind me."

"You're all law-abiding men," Reid said. "You don't want to do anything you'll be ashamed of later."

At that moment, Fanny Belle stepped out of the tent. "A hell of a lot of 'em are customers of mine, too. What the hell are they doing here, looking like the wrath of God?"

Mitch didn't look back at her. "They think you set Davis's tent on fire and tried to put a stop to his sermons."

"Hell, he can preach hellfire and damnation

every night for the rest of his life if he wants to," Fanny Belle said. "All he does is get folks excited and improve my business. Half the men that go to hear him wind up here soon as they leave there, not that I'm calling any names." She looked out at the men in the crowd. "Though I could if I was of a mind to."

The muttering in the crowd had died down quite a bit. Some of the men were looking down at their feet and shaking their heads.

"Maybe some of you men want to hear a sermon tonight," Mitch said. "A real preacher don't need a tent. He don't need a pulpit or benches. He can preach a sermon without those things. Ain't that right, Davis? Why don't you lead these men back down the street and see about what's left of that tent of yours. Make sure the ashes are cold and then preach a sermon. They'll listen. They know they need it. But this time, try preaching some sense into them."

Davis stood there like a strand of barbed wire stretched to near the breaking point. He stared at Mitch as if the preacher were wishing he still had his Bowie knife in his hand. But he didn't make a move. After a few seconds had passed, some of the tension went out of his body and he seemed to relax a little.

"The sheriff's right," he said finally. "I can preach you a sermon that'll do you good no matter where I'm standing. Because wherever I am, I'm standing on the solid rock of Jesus Christ and not the shifting sand of hypocrites. And I'll preach you a sermon tonight that'll set every foot in Paxton on the path to Glory."

He gave Mitch one last hard glance, then turned and started back down the street. The crowd parted to let him through. Some of them looked at Mitch, some at Fanny Belle. After a while, however, most of them turned to follow Davis. Of the four or five who were left, two shamefacedly walked past the sheriff and Collins to enter Fanny Belle's tent.

"Good to see that there are two honest men in town," Collins said.

Fanny Belle laughed. "A bunch of the rest of them will be back. You wait and see. And you can have anybody you want on the house, Sheriff, for what you done. If you hadn't got here with that greener, they'd have tarred and feathered me and my girls for sure. And don't think I'm forgetting you, Red. But you have girls of your own, if you want 'em. As for you, Mr. Mayor, I guess you're too good for my whores."

Reid smiled. "I'm not too good. Just too old and tired. Besides, if I'm not mistaken, I see my daughter headed this way. I don't want to set her a bad example."

"I was up at the mine," Jewel said when she reached them. "And it looks like I've missed all the excitement. What's going on here?"

"It's a long story," Reid said.

"I have time to hear it."

"I'll tell you all about it," Mitch said. "But right now it seems like it must be suppertime. This being a sheriff is hard work."

"I'll go to eat with you," Jewel said. "I'm hungry, too."

"So am I," Reid said. "What about you, Collins?"

"I'll eat at the saloon. I have to go check on things there and make sure nobody tries to cause me any trouble."

He left them, and Mitch said to Reid, "You and Jewel go on ahead. I have to ask Miss Fanny Belle a few questions."

71

"You never forget you're a sheriff, do you?" Reid said.

"Not lately," Mitch answered.

Reid smiled. "See? I told you I hired the right man for the job."

Chapter Nine

Mitch was pleased that Reid liked the way he was doing his job, even though Mitch had never intended to be a lawman. But then, he'd never really intended to be anything. He'd become a sheriff more or less by accident, if you could call it that. Whatever you called it, you couldn't call it intentional.

For years, Mitch Frye had lived a vagabond life. He had never had a real home, not even when he was a youngster living with his mother. She cared about him, but no one else around the town did. They would have been just as happy if he'd never been there. Happier probably, most of them.

As a grown man, Mitch had been a rambler. The closest he'd ever come to having roots was when he worked as a civilian scout for the Sixth Cavalry under the command of General Crook. General Phil Sheridan had eventually decided that Crook was never going to be able to keep

Geronimo on the reservation, at least not by using Apache and civilian scouts. Little Phil was a believer in total warfare in the manner of William Tecumseh Sherman. So he replaced General Crook with General Nelson Miles, who went along with Sheridan and dismissed the scouts in the belief that the Army could do its job better without them.

Cut loose from his job and the nearest thing he'd ever had to friends, Mitch had drifted in the direction of Paxton with no intention of going there until he'd had a little trouble on the trail and become a bounty hunter entirely by chance.

When he claimed the bounty in Paxton, he'd met the mayor, Mr. J. Reid Paxton himself, who had sent Mitch on another job, in the course of which Mitch had killed a man fleeing with a considerable amount of stolen money.

Paxton had tricked Mitch into signing a paper and admitting to the killing. Then Reid had used the paper to coerce Mitch into staying on in Paxton as the town's sheriff. Mitch had been furious at being fooled, but because he was a man who stuck to his agreements, he did the job that he was hired on to do. And he did it well.

After a while a funny thing had happened to Mitch. He'd begun to feel as if he belonged in Paxton. The people, most of them if not all of them, accepted him without questioning his obvious Indian heritage. Now and then men like Tolliver and Spivey came along, men who didn't like Indians and therefore didn't like Mitch simply because of his appearance. But they were the exception.

And then there was Jewel Reid. Mitch had never met a woman like her before. She didn't even seem to notice that he looked at least as much Apache as white, or if she did, she didn't care a bit.

Mitch didn't know what to make of that. He'd never really thought of meeting a respectable woman, getting married, having a home, having a family. Every now and then since he'd met Jewel, however, the possibility that he might do those things occurred to him. He wasn't comfortable with a thought like that. He knew the things Jewel would have to face if she married him, even if she didn't. And her father certainly didn't approve. He might think Mitch was a fine sheriff, but he had made it clear that he didn't want him as a son-in-law.

Not that Jewel had ever indicated that she might consider marrying him. That was just something that he had imagined. It might be that she was attracted to him simply because he was different from the other men in town. And because she liked the investigative aspect of his job, which allowed her to put her impressive mind to work on problems unlike those she dealt with in keeping the books for her father's mine.

But all those things, while they were important, occupied only a small portion of Mitch's attention. At the moment he had plenty of other things to worry about, including the questions he wanted to ask Fanny Belle.

"We can talk out here, or we can step inside," Fanny Belle said. "To tell you the truth, I wouldn't mind wetting my whistle."

Mitch said that was all right with him and followed Fanny Belle inside the tent. There were several scantily clad young women lounging around. Mitch recognized Rainbow and touched the brim of his hat. Rainbow gave him a falsely cordial smile.

"I see you two know each other," Fanny Belle said as she poured herself a glass of whiskey. "You're welcome to a free ride if you want one, Sheriff. I owe you."

"No thanks," Mitch said.

Fanny Belle held up her now full glass. "How about a drink, then?"

"I think I'll give that a pass, too."

"What's the matter, Sheriff. Don't you drink?"

"Now and then. About once a year I get drunk enough to touch the moon. But it's not time for that yet."

"Well, you let me know when you're due. I'd like to see it. Maybe then I could talk you into a little fun with one of the girls here."

"Maybe," Mitch said.

Fanny took a drink, then said, "You're a talkative son of a bitch, aren't you."

"Not so's you'd notice."

"I was just kidding, Sheriff. I guess you don't kid much, either."

"No. Not much."

"Well, hell. I guess you might as well go ahead and ask me those questions, whatever they are."

"All right, "Mitch said. "Do you know why that mob was heading for your place a while ago?"

"Sure I do. That damned preacher's been stirring them up every night about us sporting ladies. Seems he thinks the town would be better off without us. I guess he don't know what a good service we perform here. Seems to me the world would be a better place with more whores and fewer preachers, but the preachers don't see it like that."

"That's not why," Mitch told her. "Somebody said you started that fire."

Fanny Belle looked shocked. She took a deep drink and said, "Now why would anybody say that?"

"Maybe because of what you just said about how the world would be better off if there were fewer preachers."

"That's what I think, right enough. But that don't mean I'd go so far as to do anything about it. Did you ever hear of a whore running a preacher out of town?"

Mitch shook his head.

"Me, neither," Fanny Belle said. "And I don't ever expect to. It's always the other way around. And I'd bet you never heard of a whore burning down on a church. It'd be more likely that a preacher burned down a whorehouse." She took a drink, emptying her glass. "Let me tell you something, Sheriff. When it comes to downright meanness, a preacher beats a whore every single time."

"Somebody besides that preacher doesn't like having whores in this town," Mitch said.

Fanny Belle poured herself another drink and took a swallow. "Why do you say that?"

"Somebody's killed two of them."

"I mean, why do you say it's somebody besides the preacher? What makes you think it's not the preacher that's doing the killing?"

"Most preachers I've known would usually rather talk somebody to death than stick them with a knife."

"Maybe you weren't listening to what I said about preachers and meanness."

"I was listening. That doesn't mean Davis is a killer."

"He could be, though. If I were you, I wouldn't overlook him."

"I won't. Now let's get back to that question I asked you."

"What about it?"

"You never answered it."

Fanny Belle laughed. "You noticed that, huh? Well, I'll tell you the truth and shame the devil, Sheriff. I didn't set that fire. I haven't been near that preacher's tent today, and I don't intend to get near it anytime soon."

"I guess you have plenty of witnesses to say you were right here all afternoon."

"That's right. How about that, Rainbow?"

"Sure enough," Rainbow said, with a sincerity that was as false as her smile. "She was right here all the time."

Mitch knew that you could generally trust a whore to tell the truth about as much as you could trust a hungry Apache to stay on the reservation.

"Any other witnesses besides your girls?" he asked.

"Not that I can think of. My customers generally don't like to admit to the law that they were partaking of the pleasures of the flesh."

"Any idea why someone would want to blame the fire on you?"

"Didn't I ask you that already?"

"I guess maybe you did, but I thought maybe you could come up with a better answer than I could."

"Well, I can't. Unless they thought it would help get me out of town, me and all my girls. But I don't scare that easy, Sheriff, not as long as I got you and that shotgun to stand between me and them."

Mitch looked down at the shotgun that he was still holding. "I might not always be able to get here in time."

"Maybe not, but I'm betting on you." Fanny Belle finished her drink. "Sure I can't get you something?"

"No," Mitch said. "But there's something you can do for me."

"You name it."

"Tell all your girls to be extra careful tonight. Tell them not to leave here alone. They should go in pairs, at least."

"You must think I'm pretty dumb, Sheriff. But I'm not. I've already had me a little talk with the girls about that. They'll be taking a lot more care than they have been. You can count on us."

"Good," Mitch said. "That makes me feel a little better about things. So now I think I'll just go eat my supper."

Jewel and Reid were almost done with their meals when Mitch arrived at the Eat Here. Both of them were eager to hear what he'd learned from Fanny Belle, but he put them off for a minute.

Ellie West came over, and Mitch ordered steak and potatoes. Then he told Jewel and her father what he'd found out. It didn't amount to much.

"So she claims she didn't start the fire," Reid said. "I didn't think she'd admit it. Do you believe her?"

"I don't disbelieve her," Mitch told him. "She could be telling the truth, or she could be lying. With a woman like that, it's hard to tell."

"What would she have to gain from burning the tent?" Jewel asked.

"She'd let Davis know she was a dangerous woman and not somebody to be trifled with," Mitch said. "Maybe she could put a little scare into him."

"I don't think he's the kind of man that scares easily," Reid said.

Mitch agreed. "But maybe Fanny Belle doesn't know that."

Jewel said, "I'd think a woman in her profession would have to be a good judge of a man's character."

79

"How would you know that?" her father asked, his face getting redder than usual as he half rose from his chair.

"I didn't say I knew. I said I'd think that."

Reid subsided. "Oh. Well, maybe you have a point, but that doesn't make her innocent, does it, Sheriff?"

"No. But it doesn't make her guilty, either."

Reid thought about it. "Who else would start a fire like that?"

"That's a good question," Mitch said. "I wish I had an answer for it."

"Do you think there's any connection between the fire and the two dead women?" Jewel asked.

Mitch didn't know the answer to that one, either, but he was saved from trying to reply by the arrival of his steak, which was sizzling on a large white platter that Ellie slapped down in front of him.

One thing about his job, Mitch thought. It might not be easy, but he ate pretty well, even if he did have to take all his meals at the Eat Here.

"Put it on my tab," he said.

"Don't you worry," Ellie said. "It's already been done."

"What's your next step?" Reid asked when Ellie had gone.

"Eating this steak."

"Is that a joke?" Jewel asked.

"I guess it is," Mitch said after a couple of seconds.

"I don't think I've ever heard you make a joke before. Maybe there's hope for you yet."

"What's that supposed to mean?" Reid asked.

"Never mind," Jewel said. "What I want to know is how you are going to keep anyone from getting killed tonight."

Mitch sawed off a piece of steak and stuck it in

his mouth. He chewed it thoroughly, swallowed, and said, "I'm not going to do anything. I can't be everywhere. But I will stay out later and keep a close watch on things. And Fanny Belle's had a talk with her girls. They're going to be extra careful. I'll make sure Red Collins does the same thing, if he hasn't done it already."

"You think that'll work?" Reid said.

Mitch cut off another piece of steak. "I hope so," he said, "It's better than nothing. Can you think of anything better?"

"No," Reid admitted. "But it's scary to think that there's someone in Paxton who's going around killing women like that."

"And burning preachers' tents," Jewel said. "But Mitch will find out who's behind it. Isn't that right, Mitch?"

Mitch was chewing a bite of steak, so he just nodded his head. He wished he was as sure of himself as Jewel seemed to be. He didn't want anyone else to be killed.

Reid stood up. "It's time for us to be leaving."

"You go ahead," Jewel said. "I want to talk to Mitch."

It seemed for a moment that Reid would protest, but he clamped his mouth shut and stalked away.

"Now," Jewel said when he was out of earshot, "let me tell you what I think about these killings."

Chapter Ten

It was Jewel's idea that whoever was killing the women didn't really have anything against whores in particular. She thought the killer just hated women.

"And he kills the prostitutes because they're the ones he can get to the easiest," she said. "What do you think?"

They were in Mitch's office now because he hadn't wanted her to talk about the subject in the Eat Here. There were too many people there, and you could never tell who might be listening to you, even when it appeared that no one was.

"I can see what you're getting at," Mitch told Jewel. "It makes sense. Those women don't have husbands or anyone like that around, and they're out on their own when everyone else is at home asleep in bed."

"That's it. Do you think I'm right?"

"You could be. I'm not sure how it helps us, though."

"Me, neither. But it's a start."

Mitch agreed. "But I don't think your father likes the idea of you having anything to do with helping me."

"I'm sure you're right. But I'm not going to let that bother me. Are you?"

"No," Mitch said, even though he knew he was lying.

No one was killed that night, but it was a near thing. Mitch was walking toward the Bad Dog Saloon when the shooting started. There were only a few people on the streets, and all of them headed for cover when they heard the gunfire. It was coming from the direction of the burned-out tent, and Mitch started there on the run.

When he arrived, he saw that the Reverend Davis was crouched behind his charred pulpit, while most of the people who had assembled to hear him were either lying on the ground or standing rigidly with their hands in the air.

No one was moving except for a lanky individual who was stomping around the outskirts of the crowd. He had long gray hair that hung down from under his hat, and he looked a little like a preacher himself, except that instead of a Bible he was holding a Colt's Peacemaker in his right hand. He was even doing something that sounded like preaching, but the words weren't exactly the kind of thing Mitch ever expected to hear in a sermon.

"You hypocritical sons of bitches talk about the pearly gates of heaven and the streets that are paved with gold, and you say that nobody will ever be hungry or thirsty again after they cross that river Jordan. So you'd think you'd be god-damned happy to get there instead of acting like a bunch of she-goats. All I'm offering you is the chance to go to heaven sooner instead of later. Now, who wants to take me up on it?"

No one moved or spoke, which seemed to make the man even angrier. He fired a shot into the ground near the pulpit. A spout of ashes shot into the air.

"What about you, Preacher? Heaven's a beautiful place, ain't that right? Won't you have wings like an angel when you get there, and a body that don't suffer from any earthly aches and pains?"

Davis didn't answer. He just tried to scrooch down farther behind the scorched pulpit.

The man turned in a half-circle, waving his pistol. "What about the rest of you sorry bastards? You're here listening to a man who's telling about what worthless human beings you all are and what a bunch of useless sinners you've become. You can repent of all that right now, and I'll send you straight to the place you're all wanting to go. Or so you claim."

"I'm not claiming anything," Mitch said.

The man turned around and looked at him. "Where the hell did you come from?"

"Just up the street," Mitch said. "I'm the sheriff here."

"Why weren't you part of this here worshiping throng, Sheriff?"

"I was doing my job in town. Why are you causing all this trouble?"

"Because I want to show these bastards what a bunch of hypocrites they really are."

"And how are you going to do that?"

The man waggled his pistol. "You must not've heard me. I made them an offer that they ought to be glad to take me up on if they believe all they say they do. If that heaven of theirs is such a wonderful place, I'll send them there right now. No waiting around till they get any older and uglier than they already are."

"It's hard for some of us to let go of this earthly life," Mitch said. "Why don't you hand me that pistol, and I'll see that you don't get hurt."

"Who's gonna hurt me? I'm the man with the gun."

"You aren't the only one," Mitch said. "Not anymore. Have a look around."

The man looked over his shoulder and saw that half the crowd had drawn their own side arms.

"He who lives by the sword shall die by the sword," Davis said. He was now standing up and trying to look as if he hadn't been cowering under cover for the past few minutes. "The same thing is true of the gun."

"Yeah?" the lanky man said, turning toward the preacher. "Well, I think I'll just take my chances and let you take yours."

He thumbed back the hammer of his Colt, but before anyone could get off a shot, Mitch stepped up behind him and stuck the muzzle of his own pistol in the back of the man's neck. Now that he was close to him, Mitch could smell the strong odor of cheap whiskey.

"You can just hand me that pistol now," Mitch said, reaching his left hand around for it.

The man hesitated, but only for a moment. He knew when he was whipped. He put the Colt in Mitch's hand, and the sheriff stepped back and stuck it in his belt.

"Who are you, anyhow?" he asked. "I don't remember seeing you around here before."

"My name is Gabriel. And I just got here. That's my horse over there."

Mitch looked where the man pointed and saw a

horse that was about as lanky as its owner, though it was obviously well cared for.

"Gabriel?" Mitch said. "Are you sure that's your real name?"

"My mother always called me Gabe, but I was given to understand that was short for Gabriel. Maybe she thought I'd grow up to be an angel. If she did, she missed her guess."

"I'd say she did, at that," Mitch agreed. Then he said to Davis, "Preacher, you can go on with your services now. If anybody gets to heaven tonight, it won't be any thanks to Gabriel here."

If Mitch was expecting any thanks from Davis, he didn't get it, though several of the men nearby murmured their appreciation. Mitch spotted Sam Neely and stopped to ask him to take care of Gabriel's horse.

"I'll see that he pays," Mitch said. "And if he doesn't, the mayor will stand good for it."

"You sure of that?" Neely asked.

"I'm sure," Mitch said, and he took Gabriel off to the jail.

The town was quiet for the rest of the night, and Mitch spent most of it standing in the shadows of the alleys near Fanny Belle's place. There was no sign of anyone lurking there, lying in wait for one of the whores to come along alone.

If there had been, he would have been frustrated by the fact that the women stuck together, leaving their places of business in twos and threes. And as far as Mitch could tell, none of the women who worked at Bad Dog left at all. A couple of hours before dawn, he went back to his room and slept the rest of the night.

The next morning after breakfast, Mitch went to check on his prisoner. Gabriel was sitting on his cot, holding his head in his hands. He looked up when Mitch tapped on the bars. The whites of his eyes were shot through with red lines.

"Feeling a little ragged?" Mitch asked.

"Pretty damned ragged," Gabriel answered. "Where am I?"

"Jail," Mitch said.

"Figured. Mind telling me why?"

Mitch told him.

"Damn. I can't remember a thing about it. I'm sorry I acted up like that, Sheriff. I do it now and then. My brother's a preacher, and I get mighty tired of his holier-than-thou stuff. My mother always used to make small of me because I wasn't like him. I got so I hated that woman. And my brother, too. Sometimes I take it out on other folks."

"And last night you took it out on the ones here."

"If you say so. I don't remember it. My head feels about the size of this mountain we're sitting on."

"I guess you won't be wanting any breakfast, then."

"I'd as soon not think about eating, if it's all the same to you."

"I don't mind," Mitch said. "If you don't eat, the town will save a little money. And speaking of money, I had your horse stabled over night. You're going to owe for it."

"All right. Any other fines?"

"I should probably charge you something, but we don't have any judge here to set the fines, and I don't want to cheat you. I'll let you go now if you think you can keep out of trouble."

"You don't have to worry about that. I'll just ride back down your mountain and right on out of your life."

"Sounds like a good idea," Mitch said.

"I do have one little piece of advice for you, though," Gabriel said.

"What?"

Gabriel reached down to his boot and pulled out a knife as long and wicked looking as the one Davis had used on the tent ropes.

"You really ought to search your prisoners better," Gabriel said. "You never know what a man might be carrying in his boot."

Mitch realized that he wasn't as good a sheriff as Reid had thought. He'd gotten careless, and it was lucky that he was still alive.

"I'll remember that," he said.

He unlocked the door, and Gabriel stood up, a trifle unsteadily.

"You think you can make it to the livery stable?" Mitch asked.

"You just point me in the right direction. I can find it."

Mitch led Gabriel outside. He returned the man's pistol to him and showed him where the stable was located. Gabriel walked in that direction, staggering only slightly. Mitch wondered just how much whiskey the man had drunk. It must have been a lot.

Mitch had planned to spend the day questioning some of the people who had responded so avidly to Davis's sermons, but the knife concealed in Gabriel's boot had set him to thinking. He went back to his office and read over the list he'd made earlier. Then he folded it carefully, put it in a drawer, and started a new one.

1. Who started the fire at Davis's tent? Could Davis have started it himself? Didn't seem all that interested in putting it out. If he started it, why?

2. Jewel thinks the killer hates women. Davis doesn't like them.
3. Davis had a Bowie knife in his boot. Women were killed with a knife. Ellie West—plenty of knives in Eat Here. O'Connor—knives at store. Bill Carson? George Kelley?

He stopped his list right there. He could think of reasons that Carson might carry a knife, but Kelley was a banker. It didn't seem likely that he'd have a knife on him.

But did either of them hate women? What about O'Connor? And what about Ellie West. She was a woman herself. She wouldn't have any reason to hate other women, would she?

There was just too much going on, and too much to think about. Mitch was still trying to make sense of things when Jewel came in.

"Shouldn't you be at work?" he asked her.

"I'm the boss's daughter," Jewel said. "I can come and go as I please, as long as the work gets done on time and as long as it's done right."

Mitch had a feeling that Jewel would do any job right if she set out to do it in the first place, though he didn't say so.

She glanced down at the new list he'd made and picked it up to read it. He didn't bother to stop her. She could do pretty much as she pleased around him, just as she could around her father.

"You have plenty of suspects," she said after she'd finished reading.

"More than I need."

He thought for a minute. Then he jumped out of his chair and ran through the door.

"What's the matter?" Jewel yelled after him. "Where are you going?"

Mitch didn't slow down. "The matter is I'm an

idiot," he called over his shoulder. "And I'm going to the livery stable."

Jewel didn't ask why. She simply followed him, but at a more sedate pace.

Sam Neely had a small blacksmithing operation, and he was beating a hot wagon wheel into shape when Mitch got to the stable. The hammer rang against the iron of the wheel and the anvil. When Neely saw Mitch, he looked at the wheel critically, then plunged it into a trough of water, which bubbled and hissed.

"What the devil's your hurry?" he asked Mitch.

"That fella I arrested last night," Mitch said. "Where is he?"

"Long gone," Neely answered. "He paid up and left about a half hour ago."

"God damn," Mitch said.

Jewel walked into the livery stable just then. "Such language."

"Beg your pardon," Mitch said. "I didn't know you were here."

"I'm not as fast as you are, but I can cover the distance. What are you so angry about, anyway?"

Mitch said, "I think I just let our killer get away."

"You mean that man that shot up the preaching last night?" Neely said. "The one that just got his horse back from me?"

"That's the one," Mitch told him.

"God damn," Neely said.

Chapter Eleven

While Neely was saddling Mitch's horse, the sheriff told Jewel what had occurred to him and made him run out of the office.

"He practically told me he was the killer," Mitch said, shaking his head. "He pulled his knife out of his boot and showed it to me."

"Did he say he'd used it?" Jewel asked.

"He didn't have to. He must've decided by then I was about as smart as that wagon wheel Neely was working on. He was taunting me with it. Look, he shot up the services on the same day somebody set the tent on fire. He's carrying a knife that'd do the job that was done on those whores. He hates preachers, and he hates women." Mitch paused. "Well, he hates one woman, anyhow. That might be enough."

"So you really think he's the one?"

"He must be. And I let him out of jail so he

could walk right down here to the livery, get on his horse, and ride out of town."

"There's a good side to it," Jewel said. "If you look at it the right way."

"I'm glad you can see it," Mitch said. "I sure can't."

"If he's gone, he won't be killing anyone else."

"Not here, he won't. But what about wherever he goes from here? It was my job to put a stop to him, and I didn't do it."

Neely came up, leading Mitch's horse. "Ready to go, Sheriff."

"Any other horses been out of here this morning besides my prisoner's?"

"Nope. Why?"

"Tracks," Mitch said, kneeling down to examine the ground.

He saw the fresh tracks immediately and fixed them firmly in his mind. If there was anything Mitch was good at, it was tracking. He could follow Gabriel anywhere now.

"You don't really know he's the right man," Jewel said, but Mitch was already in the saddle.

"His name's Gabriel," he said.

"Like the angel?" Jewel asked.

"Avenging angel," Mitch said, and rode out.

There was only one road into Paxton, and if you wanted to leave, you had to take the same road out. Of course, the road did run in two directions. You could go on up the mountain to where the mines were, places with names like the Elbow Grease and the Lucky Man and the Rocky Den. But the road played out when the mines did, and all that was left after that was the top of the mountain.

Mitch didn't think Gabriel would have gone that way. He might have been able to get to the top of the mountain and down the other side, but as far as Mitch knew there was no sign of a trail. It would be rough traveling, and there was no reason for Gabriel to risk it.

The other way out of town was down the same road that came into it. Gabriel could have gotten off the road, but again the traveling would have been rough. Not as rough as the other way, however, since some of the people coming up or going down had one reason or another not to stick with the road and had made some side trails. But Gabriel didn't have any reason to think that Mitch was following after him, so he would most likely stay with the relatively smooth going of the road.

That proved to be the case. Mitch found the tracks in the street and saw that they led out of town, down the mountain. Mitch followed them. On his way out of town, he saw several people he knew, including O'Connor, who should have been at his store; Bill Carson, who should have been up at Paxton's mine; and the Reverend Davis, who was standing near the remains of his tent in close conversation with Herman Tolliver. The next thing you knew, Mitch thought, Tolliver would be getting himself baptized.

Mitch passed by the burned tent and looked back. J. Reid Paxton was riding after him.

"Where the hell do you think you're going?" Paxton called.

"After a killer," Mitch said.

"What about the town? You can't just leave like you didn't have a job to do here."

"If you're worried about me coming back, you don't have to. You still got that paper on me."

"I'm not worried about that. I'm worried about what might happen while you're gone."

Mitch reined in his horse and thought about

that. He said, "Those women got killed when I was in town. Now I got to stop the one who did it from killing somebody else."

"That's what Jewel said, but you don't even know for sure this Gabriel's the man you want."

"I'm sure enough," Mitch said, nudging his horse into motion. "I'll be back as soon as I can."

Paxton sat there staring at his back, and Mitch rode on out of town. It would take Gabriel most of the day to get to the bottom of the mountain, Mitch figured. He didn't seem to be in any hurry. It was clear from the tracks that his horse was just walking. Mitch might be able to overtake him before he got to the bottom.

That would be the best thing. If he got off the mountain, Gabriel could go in any direction at all, and while Mitch was confident of his ability to pick up the man's trail, it might take him a while. Long enough, in fact, to give Gabriel such a head start that it would take Mitch days to catch up with him. Mitch didn't want that to happen, and he urged his own mount to pick up the pace. He didn't want to overdo it, however. That would be careless and dangerous, and he didn't want to take a chance of hurting his horse and losing Gabriel completely.

On the road down, Mitch passed a couple of people who were coming up the mountain. He stopped them both and asked if they'd seen Gabriel.

"Tall feller with gray hair?" the first man asked. "I seen him, all right. He stopped and asked me if I had any whiskey on me."

"Did you?" Mitch asked.

"Not that I was gonna give any to some sorry son of a bitch I met on the road. I keep it for my own drinkin'."

Mitch thanked the man and went on his way.

As he rode, he thought of something else that Gabriel had said, about not remembering anything that he might have done the night before. Mitch had heard of people who had blank places in their memories after a night of hard drinking, and if Gabriel was telling the truth about that, it was even possible that he didn't remember killing the whores. Mitch wasn't really sure that was possible, and even if it was, it didn't excuse what Gabriel had done. He had to be stopped before he did it again.

Mitch was thinking about how to stop him when the bullet whizzed by his nose. It was followed almost at once by the flat crack of a rifle shot.

Mitch stopped thinking and let his body take over. He rolled off his horse and hit the ground. Another bullet buzzed by, zinging off a nearby rock about the size of a grizzly. Mitch scrambled for the rock, which was the nearest cover.

He didn't quite make it. Something struck him a hard blow in the right foot and sent him sprawling. He could feel the skin peeling off his hands as he skidded forward.

Luckily, his skid brought him so near the rock that all he had to do was roll behind it. He didn't take time to analyze his wounds. He drew his Colt and snapped off a couple of shots over the top of the rock without rising up to see where he was shooting. All he hoped to do was give the rifleman, who he figured must be Gabriel, something to think about.

The answering bullet whined off the top of the rock near Mitch's head, taking out a big chip of stone, but it didn't come close to Mitch, who wondered how the hell Gabriel had figured out there was someone after him. There had been no sign of Gabriel's turning back, so he must have turned farther on down the mountain. Far enough down to keep Mitch from realizing that he was about to be ambushed.

Mitch wasn't worried about getting hit as long as the shooter stayed where he was. The rock gave plenty of cover. Of course, the shooter knew that too, and he might very well try to move and get a better shot.

Mitch decided he'd better take stock of himself. He looked down at his foot. It didn't hurt, which wasn't surprising. Getting shot didn't hurt at first. It took a while for the shock to wear off. That's when the pain started.

But Mitch wasn't going to have any pain, not from his foot. There was no blood at all, and Mitch grinned when he saw that the heel had been shot off his boot. That was why he'd been tripped up. Getting your boot heel shot off was enough to knock you off balance, and the impact had sure been hard enough to fool Mitch into thinking the bullet had actually hit him.

In fact, the worst thing that had happened to Mitch was the fall. The heels of both hands were skinned and bloody, with dirt and gravel embedded in the tender flesh. It stung, but it wasn't serious.

Mitch thought about what he could do.

He could jump up and get himself shot. That would be easy, but it wouldn't be smart. Mitch didn't have any desire to die, not right then.

He could try to outflank Gabriel and slip around behind him. It sounded good, but there was no cover nearby aside from the rock. He'd get shot as soon as he made a move.

He could also just sit right where he was and let Gabriel be the one who tried to do the flanking movement. He'd be taking a chance, but it wasn't as big a chance as the other two choices, and maybe he could spot Gabriel and get off a shot at him. Besides, there didn't seem to be any other possibility.

So Mitch replaced the two cartridges he'd fired and sat back to wait.

He waited for what he figured was about an hour. No one passed on the road, and there were no further shots in his direction. He kept a close eye out in all directions that he could see, and he couldn't detect any movement in the trees other than that of a few songbirds and a couple of red squirrels.

That's when he realized he'd been fooled again.

Mitch's horse hadn't wandered far, and he caught it easily, or anyway as easily as it was possible for a man who was missing the heel of his right boot. By the time he got into the saddle, Mitch was so angry with himself that his ears were burning. He told himself to calm down, and to help himself along he rolled a cigarette and smoked it.

It helped, but not much. Mitch was beginning to feel like the biggest fool of the year. Gabriel hadn't needed to kill him, though that might have been his original plan. But what he'd done had probably worked out just about as well. He'd put Mitch behind a rock for an hour, while he got a good, fast head start down the mountain. It was going to be that much harder for Mitch to catch up with him, and it would be even more complicated now that Gabriel knew he was being followed.

Mitch cussed and pinched the coal off the end of his smoke. He was going to get Gabriel or know the reason why.

He hadn't ridden very far when he met a man on a mule, coming fast. That mule could flat out run, especially considering that it was going uphill.

"Whoa, mule!" the man said, hauling back on the reins when he spotted Mitch. "Whoa, you hammerheaded son of a bitch!"

The mule stopped and the man looked at Mitch, who looked right back. He couldn't really tell what the man looked like. He had a shaggy beard that covered his face so completely that all Mitch could really see were his eyes, which were black and shiny.

"That a badge you're wearing?" the man asked.

"That's right."

The man's eyes narrowed. "I didn't know there was any sheriff around these parts."

"I'm new on the job," Mitch said.

"I don't guess that matters none. And speakin' of jobs, I got one for you."

"I already have one," Mitch told him.

"It's not that kind of a job. What I mean is that I got something to show you that's a job for a lawman. Tell you the truth, I'm mighty glad I run across you."

"What kind of job are you talking about?" Mitch asked.

The man jerked a thumb over his shoulder. "Dead man."

Mitch didn't quite get his meaning. "Dead man?"

"That's right. Dead man. There's one down the road about a mile."

"Goddamn," Mitch said. He wondered who Gabriel had killed this time.

The man told Mitch that his name was Alky. "I don't drink the stuff, though. I used to make it and sell it. But now I've come to stake a claim and make me a fortune in mining."

Mitch didn't think there was much likelihood of that. "How'd you happen to spot the dead man?" he asked.

"Happened when I stopped to take a piss," Alky said. "He was lyin' in the brush. I nearly pissed right on his head, by God. I don't know about you, but I'm kinda delicate about somethin' like that. I mean, the man's dead, and it don't mean nothin' to him, but it don't seem right, somehow. Pissin' on a man's head, I mean. Don't matter if he's dead. You ought not do somethin' like that to him."

"Did you piss on his head?"

"Hell, no. When I saw that it was a dead man, it scared me so bad my stream cut itself right off. It was five minutes before I could get it started again, and by then I wasn't anywhere close to the dead man. It was a mighty painful piss, I'll say that. Burned like hell. I guess it was because it cut off like that when I got nervy."

Mitch didn't have any comment to make on that score. He asked if Alky had seen the dead man's horse.

"Not a hide nor a hair. He had one, though. I seen the tracks. Somebody took it, or it run off, one or the other." He pointed along the road. "We're just about there. That little patch of brush up ahead."

Alky hadn't gone far off the road to take his piss, for which Mitch didn't blame him. There weren't that many travelers on the road, and Alky didn't strike Mitch as the shy type anyhow.

Mitch stopped and dismounted. When he walked over to the brush, he looked down and saw the body.

It was Gabriel.

Chapter Twelve

Now that Alky wasn't in such a rush, he was able to locate Gabriel's horse off in the trees. He caught him up while Mitch was having a look at Gabriel's body, but the horse was a little shy, and it took Alky a while to coax him to come.

While Alky was trying to coax the horse, Mitch stared down Gabriel, who had been shot in the chest with a rifle. Probably the bullet had struck him in the heart, or near enough to it to knock off a piece of it. That's all it would take to kill a man dead as a hammer.

Mitch knelt down and touched Gabriel's throat. He was already cold, which meant that he'd been dead awhile. Mitch hadn't heard any shots, but he figured that Gabriel had been killed while Mitch was on his way down the mountain, before he'd spent an hour waiting behind a rock for a bullet that never came. What with the curves in the road and all the rocks and trees in between where

Gabriel was and where Mitch had come from, it was likely that Mitch wouldn't have heard a thing.

Mitch thought about it. It was possible that someone Gabriel had met on the road hadn't liked his looks and had decided to kill him. But it seemed more probable that someone had followed Gabriel down the mountain from town. Mitch thought it was also likely that whoever had followed Gabriel had avoided the road, not wanting to be seen, and had been riding off to the side. Maybe after bushwhacking Gabriel, that someone had seen Mitch and thought it might be a good idea to kill him, too.

Mitch stood up and brushed dirt off the knees of his Levi's. He'd obviously been completely wrong about Gabriel. Or maybe not. Maybe someone had discovered what Gabriel had done and decided to get a little private revenge.

But if that were true, why take a shot at Mitch? The whole situation was getting a little too complicated for Mitch. He'd have to take some time and sort through everything, but right now he had other things to do.

He examined the ground carefully for tracks, and after a few minutes he located the tracks of a horse that he figured must have been Gabriel's.

"Want to sling him up on his horse?" Alky asked. He had brought the horse over to the side of the road and was standing there scratching in his beard. "Mighty good-looking horse. Good-natured, too. What happens to a feller's horse after he's dead?"

Mitch didn't know the answer to that. When he'd killed the outlaws whose heads he carried to Paxton for bounty, he'd sold their horses and pocketed the money, but that didn't seem quite right in this case. On the other hand, if Alky was hinting that he'd like to have the horse, he was out of luck.

"I'll sell the horse and use the money to bury him, unless he's carrying some ready cash," Mitch said.

Alky scratched some more. "Be a little left over. 'Specially if you sell that saddle. Pretty nice saddle."

Mitch was tired of talking money. He walked over and checked the horse's tracks. Sure enough, they matched the ones near Gabriel's body. Now he had to see if he could locate the tracks of another horse. That could take a long time, considering that Mitch had no idea where the rider had been when Gabriel had been shot.

Mitch looked around, scanning the area for a likely spot to set up an ambush. There were plenty of places. The trouble was picking the best one.

"You gonna leave that feller lyin' there all day?" Alky asked.

"We'll take care of him in a minute," Mitch said. "I want to see if I can find out where his killer was sitting."

Alky pointed to a spot just down the road where a large rock lay next to several trees growing out of the mountainside about ten feet higher than the road.

"I'd say you oughta have a look right over there. Man could tie his horse in the trees, stand behind that rock, and get a nice clear shot at anybody riding down the road."

Mitch agreed that it was a good place to set up. He walked down the road, navigating awkwardly thanks to the missing boot heel, and had a look. It was a good spot, all right. Mitch found an empty brass cartridge on the ground near the rock, and he found where the horse had been tied. He memorized the horse's tracks, though he didn't intend to follow them. He was sure that as soon as they got close to town, the rider would get on the road and mingle with other riders. Soon his horse's tracks would be lost among all the others.

Mitch walked back to where Alky was standing beside Gabriel's body.

"Help me lift him up," Mitch said. "I have to take him into town and make some arrangements."

With Alky's help, Mitch picked up the body and tossed Gabriel over his own saddle. He wasn't heavy, but he was an awkward load.

"Reckon there oughta be some kinda reward for finding a dead man," Alky said. "Helpin' out the law and all that."

"You're not getting his saddle or his horse," Mitch told him. "But I appreciate your help."

" 'Preciatin' don't set the table."

Mitch mounted his own horse. "I thought you were going to make your fortune in the mines."

Alky climbed on his mule. "Well, now, I been thinkin' about that. I don't know as I'm suited to that kinda work. And it might be that all the good claims is already taken."

Mitch thought Alky was probably right about that. There weren't many people getting rich in Paxton, except for J. Reid Paxton himself. One or two others had made some fair strikes, but a newcomer didn't really stand much of a chance.

"You don't need yourself a deputy, by any chance?" Alky asked.

"You know anything about being a lawman?"

"Nope. Never even been arrested."

"I'll think about it," Mitch said.

After a little side trip, they arrived in town, leading the horse with Gabriel's body slung across it.

There were curious stares, but no one was interested enough to ask any questions.

No one, that is, except J. Reid Paxton, who showed up at Evan Riley's place before Mitch even had the body off the horse. Paxton seemed to appear at Mitch's elbow whenever anything happened. He must have eyes and ears all over the place, Mitch thought.

"Who is it?" Paxton asked.

"Gabriel," Mitch said. "The man I was following."

"So he was the one."

"The one what?" Alky asked.

Paxton looked at him. "Who're you?"

"That's Alky," Mitch said. "He wants to be my deputy. I told him I'd think about it."

"You meant *I'd* think about it," Paxton said.

Mitch gave him a level look. "I guess I meant *we'd* think about it."

Paxton's face reddened, but he took a deep breath before he spoke, and his voice came out calmly.

"You're right. We'll think about it. Now, what about Gabriel? Is he the one who killed the whores?"

"What whores?" Alky wanted to know.

"You keep quiet," Paxton told him. "We'll fill you in later. Maybe. What about it, Frye?"

Mitch shook his head. "I don't know."

Paxton looked shocked. "You killed him, and you don't know?"

"That's the problem," Mitch said. "I didn't kill him."

"Damn," Paxton said. "If you didn't, who did?"

"We're working on that," Alky said.

"That's right," Mitch said. "We're working on it."

* * *

Back in his office, Mitch stared at a blank piece of paper, but he didn't write anything on it. He didn't know what to write.

Beside the paper on top of his desk were most of Gabriel's worldly possessions: a cheap pocket watch that didn't run, a five-dollar gold piece, a knife, and a pistol. His bedroll, camping gear, and saddlebags with a change of clothes were at Sam Neely's, but there was nothing of value there.

Who would have wanted to kill Gabriel? Mitch could think of only one person with any kind of reason, and that was the Reverend Davis. But Mitch had seen Davis before leaving town. Davis couldn't have gotten ahead of Mitch and caught up with Gabriel.

Or could he? Mitch had been delayed by his conversation with Reid. Davis would have had a chance to get ahead if he'd made a real effort, as unlikely as that seemed.

What really bothered Mitch about everything that had happened was that he felt he'd seen or heard something that might put him on the right road to an answer, something that was the key to the whole thing, but he couldn't for the life of him think what it might be.

Alky came through the door of the office and interrupted Mitch's train of thought.

"Well?" he asked.

"Well, what?" Mitch said.

"What did you and Mr. Paxton decide about me hirin' on as your deputy?"

Mitch put the blank paper in a desk drawer and looked at Alky. He was no more than two inches over five feet, he was bandy-legged, and he didn't even carry a gun. He was about the most improbable deputy Mitch could imagine.

But to Mitch's surprise, Paxton had thought Mitch could use a little help around the office and the jail.

"This man, what did you say his name was?" Paxton had asked.

"Alky."

"Alky. Interesting name. Well, he could clean the place up, and he could probably even do some patrolling for you during the quiet part of the day."

Mitch thought that was a good idea. He didn't mind cleaning out the office and the jail, but it would be better to have his time free for more important things.

"What about pay?"

"He won't need much," Paxton said. "Half a dollar a day. And he can get his meals at the Eat Here. He'll have to find his own place to stay."

Mitch had no intention of sharing his own small quarters with anyone. There was hardly room for him.

"How about the jail?" he asked.

"It doesn't bother me, as long as it doesn't bother your deputy. And as long as there's room."

Reid had let it go at that, and allowed Mitch to make the final decision. So Mitch told Alky what they'd decided.

Alky wasn't impressed. "Hell, I could do better if I was to try minin'."

"Think about those free meals," Mitch said. "And then think about eating your own cooking all the time."

"You got a point there," Alky said.

"And you'll be sleeping inside, even if it is inside a jail. You won't have to worry about staking a claim, building a lean-to, or any of that."

"You convinced me," Alky said. "I'll take the job."

So now Mitch had a deputy. It was time to put him to work.

"You can go swamp out the jail," he told Alky. "It's Saturday. We'll probably be having a crowd in there tonight."

Alky had heard about the Reverend Davis. "Won't ever'body be at the preachin'?"

"I think folks might be getting a little tired of preaching."

"What about them whores?" Alky asked. "You gonna tell me about that?"

So Mitch told him the whole story, as best he could piece it together. He didn't try to put any of his own speculations in, just related the events more or less as they'd happened.

"Goddamn," Alky said when Mitch was finished. "Sounds to me like you got some kinda crazy man runnin' loose here in Paxton. Maybe I shoulda asked about those whores *before* I took the job."

"Maybe you should've," Mitch agreed. "But you didn't. If you're having second thoughts, you can quit right now. That's probably the smart thing to do, and I won't hold it against you."

"I ain't a quitter. When I take a job, I like to stick to it."

"You may be sorry," Mitch said.

"I expect you're right," Alky said. "I prob'ly will."

Chapter Thirteen

Mitch was right about Saturday night. While a number of the miners were still interested enough to attend the Reverend Davis's services, most of them were much more interested in indulging in their usual Saturday-night activities, which included all the things Davis was preaching against and probably a few that Davis hadn't even thought of yet.

Alky went with Mitch on his rounds and was introduced all around the town as the new deputy. The only thing Mitch had given him from Gabriel's possessions was the pistol, with which Alky showed some familiarity.

"I don't carry one, but that don't mean I can't use one. I just always figgered that if I had one on me, it'd cause me about as much trouble as it'd keep away."

Mitch didn't say so, but he thought Alky might

be correct in his figuring. He was turning out to be a lot smarter than he looked.

Alky seemed to enjoy his status as deputy, and he told everyone he met that he was the one who'd found Gabriel's body. Most people had already heard the story, since stories like that had a way of getting around town in a very short time, but Alky embellished it enough to make it interesting.

He particularly embellished it for Fanny Belle, who was clearly impressed and who even offered Alky a free ride with any girl in the house.

"No charge. A brave man like you deserves a little fun," she told him.

"How about it, Sheriff?" he asked, turning hopefully to Mitch. "What's the policy of the law?"

"No free rides," Mitch said. "The law can't afford to be beholden to anybody."

"Goddang it, I knew it. I knew I shoulda taken up minin' instead of lawin'."

Alky had plenty of other reasons to wish he'd taken up mining before the evening was over. Mitch had him climb up on the roof of the bank and get a drunk down before the man fell and broke his neck.

The drunk turned out to be a miner named Haskins, and he'd apparently decided to rob the place by cutting a hole in the roof and climbing through, but he couldn't do the job with just his Barlow knife. Whether he could do what he set out to or not, Haskins hadn't wanted to come down, and he and Alky had gotten into a scuffle that had nearly resulted in both of them falling into the alley. Alky had finally subdued Haskins by getting a choke hold on him.

"What'll we do with him?" Alky asked when he

finally had Haskins safely back on solid ground. "I'd shoot him if it was up to me."

Mitch agreed that it might be a good idea, but it didn't fit with the way he'd been enforcing the law in Paxton. So they half-walked, half-carried Haskins to jail and tossed him into a cell. Haskins was snoring loudly before they got the cell door shut.

After that episode, Alky and Mitch had to stop a man from killing one of Fanny Belle's girls he believed had taken money from his pants while he was distracted. The man had been belligerent at first, insisting that he'd been robbed, but then he'd simply turned tail and run, tearing out of the place wearing nothing but his long johns. Alky had to chase him down the street and tackle him.

He eventually admitted that he hadn't been robbed at all. He'd been short of money to pay for his pleasure, and he'd thought maybe he could turn the tables and get out without paying anything.

"No free rides," Alky told him. "If I don't get one, you sure as hell don't."

They took him to the jail and put him in the cell with Haskins to let him get whatever rest he could with the roof-crawling bank robber still snoring away like a hog snuffling through the mud looking for an ear of corn.

Most unsettling of all, they had to break up three serious fights, the worst of which occurred in the Bad Dog Saloon. Five or six men playing stud poker got into a disagreement about the dealer's honesty, in the course of which words were exchanged, punches were thrown, and shots were fired.

Mitch and Alky had just finished putting their latest prisoner in his cell when they heard the shots. By the time they arrived at the Bad Dog, a full-scale brawl was in progress, involving practically every man in the saloon and a couple of the women, one of whom was riding a man on the back while pounding him on the head with a whiskey glass. The man refused to go down, though blood was flying from the lacerations on his scalp.

Red Collins met Mitch at the entrance. His coat was torn, and there was a red mark where someone had hit him high up on his right cheek.

"At least they've stopped shooting and started trying to kill each other with their bare hands," he said. "I hope you can stop them before they wreck the place."

"Looks like they already got a good start," Alky said, dodging aside as a man came staggering past to fall facedown on the boardwalk.

"We'll see what we can do," Mitch said. "Let's go, Alky."

They waded into the mob, pulling the combatants apart when they could and using a judicious measure of force where necessary, usually by applying the barrel of a pistol to some part of a man's head.

It took a few minutes, but they finally restored something resembling order. There were five men lying unconscious on the floor, and another was atop the bar.

"I think he just went to sleep," the bartender said. "Nobody hit him, not as far as I could see."

Finding out who'd started the fray was impossible, and Mitch had just about decided to forget about it and let everyone off the hook when someone said, "Ain't no goddamn Indian gonna put me in jail."

Mitch looked at the man, who was well over six feet tall and easily the biggest man in the saloon. The place was very quiet now, the loudest noise being the heavy breathing of the men who were recovering from their recent exertions. The man sleeping on the bar rolled over to get into a more comfortable position.

Mitch looked at the man who'd spoken. "I guess you mean me."

"Goddamn right I mean you. Who else would I be talking about? I don't see no other Indians in here, do you?"

"Did you start this fight?"

"What the hell difference does that make? I ain't going anywhere with you whether I did or not."

"Sounds like a confession to me," Alky said. He didn't look any the worse for all the scuffling, except that there was a little blood in his beard. Not his, as he told Mitch later. "I'd arrest him if I was you, Sheriff."

"Who the hell are you?" the man asked.

"I'm the deputy. Who the hell are you?"

"I'm Rip Bowman, and I say no Indian is arresting me, not even if he has some scraggly deputy to help him out."

"I've changed my mind," Alky said. "I don't think you should arrest him, Sheriff. I think you should kill him."

Bowman said, "You're the one who's gonna get killed, you Indian-loving little turd." Then he made a jump for Alky.

He was big enough to have flattened the little deputy if he'd landed on him, but Alky wasn't just smarter than he looked. He was also quicker. He dodged to the side and left Bowman grabbing for air.

"The big 'uns is always clumsy," Alky said. "You can go ahead and shoot him now, Sheriff."

Bowman turned to look at Mitch, who still hadn't drawn his pistol. While Bowman's back was turned, Alky stood in a chair and laid the barrel of his pistol across the back of Bowman's skull. The big man made an inarticulate noise and fell on his face with a thud and a crunching sound.

"I 'spect that was his nose breakin'," Alky said. "Not that I give much of a damn if it was."

"Me neither," Collins said. "All I care about is getting him out of my place of business. I think everyone else just wants to have a peaceful good time." He looked around the saloon. "That right, boys?"

His question was answered by a few enthusiastic shouts of "Damn right, Red" from those who still felt like shouting. Most of the others were still too stunned to say anything.

"Let's haul him out of here, then," Mitch said.

He and Alky each took an arm and dragged Bowman to the jail, the toes of his boots making two little trails in the street.

"Drag him through some of them horse apples over there," Alky said, giving a tug to the right, but Mitch persuaded him that wasn't a good idea.

"We got one in there snoring already. No need to stink the place up. You might be sleeping there."

"Forgot about that for a minute," Alky said. "Never mind the horse apples."

They put Bowman in a cell to himself and went into Mitch's office for a smoke. Mitch rolled a cigarette, and Alky brought out a beat-up old corncob pipe from somewhere inside his shirt.

After he stuffed the pipe with tobacco and got it going, Alky said, "You have to put up with that kind of stuff often?"

"What kind of stuff?" Mitch asked.

"You know what I mean. That Injun stuff."

Mitch thought about Spivey and Tolliver and

about all the others like them he'd met over the years.

"Often enough," he said.

"You don't really look Injun, not to anybody's been around 'em much. 'Course, I guess you know that."

Mitch nodded. "I know that."

"Ain't what Bowman meant, anyhow. He prob'ly wouldn't care if you was a full-blood Injun. That wouldn't bother him near as much as what you are."

"I know that, too."

"Figgered you did." Alky drew on his pipe and let a cloud of white smoke drift out of his mouth. "Bother you to talk about it?"

Mitch didn't know how he felt. He'd never talked about his mixed blood with anyone before, not in any civilized way. Usually the discussions went something along the lines of the one they'd just had with Bowman and ended about the same.

"I'm not sure," Mitch said.

"Don't have to talk about it if you don't want to. I'm just a nosy old man."

"You're not old. Those whiskers of yours might fool a man for a while, but nobody who can climb around on a roof like you did and coldcock a rowdy like Bowman is much older than I am. And I'm not an old man."

"Well, maybe I ain't neither. But I feel old as the goddamed hills sometimes,'specially when I run into sonsabitches like that Bowman. I guess you met plenty more like him back when you was comin' up."

"Yeah," Mitch said. "Plenty."

"Bet you didn't let 'em buffalo you, though."

"No," Mitch said. "I didn't."

He'd been in many a fight, and he'd come out

the loser in some of them, but he'd never backed away.

"Mitch Frye," Alky said. "That ain't no Injun name."

"Frye's my mother's name," Mitch said. "I never knew my father."

Alky let out smoke. "I never knew mine, neither, but I guess he wasn't no Injun."

"Be hard to tell, all those whiskers on your face."

"Yep. Hard to tell how old I am or how ugly I am, too. Whiskers is good for a lot of things."

"Reckon I should grow me some?" Mitch asked.

"Always heard tell you Injuns couldn't raise a beard. That true?"

"Not in my case," Mitch said, rubbing the stubble on his chin. "I have to shave every day."

"Not worth the trouble, if you ask me, which I don't guess you did. Is it 'bout time to go walk the streets again?"

"It's late and things have quieted down. You can go get some sleep. I'll do whatever needs to be done."

Alky tapped his pipe against his boot heel, knocking ashes on the floor.

"You'll have to sweep those up tomorrow," Mitch said.

"I don't mind. I mind havin' to sleep in the same jail with that Bowman, though."

"You'll get used to him."

"I don't think I'll ever get used to the likes of him," Alky said. "I bet you never have."

"No," Mitch said. "I never have."

Alky had been gone for about an hour when Red Collins came by.

115

"I just wanted to thank you," Collins said. "I'd have lost the whole place if you and your deputy hadn't showed up. Hiring you was the smartest thing Reid's done since he elected himself mayor."

Mitch never knew how to respond to compliments, maybe because he'd had so few of them. He said, "You could have handled it. It might have taken you longer, but you could have got it under control."

"I don't think so," Collins said. "But that's not the only reason I'm here. There's something I forgot to tell you. That man you killed, Gabriel. He was in my place the other night, and he got into an argument with one of the girls, I thought I was going to have to call for them. But he left before things got out of hand."

"What kind of argument?" Mitch asked.

"Now, that's a funny thing. He was talking to her like he was a preacher. Told her that she was disgusting and a disgrace to womanhood."

"His brother was a preacher, so he told me. Must be some of it rubbed off on him."

"Could be. I heard from Reid you thought he killed those women, and I just wanted to let you know how he talked."

"I appreciate that," Mitch said.

"And I appreciate what you did tonight. Come in tomorrow and have a drink on the house."

"I'll think about it," Mitch said.

Chapter Fourteen

The next morning Mitch sat in his office with his blank piece of paper. He was trying to think of what to write on it when Jewel walked in.

"You didn't come to breakfast," she said. "But your new deputy did. You seem to have had a busy day yesterday."

"You could say that."

"And you didn't tell me about any of it. I had to find out from my father. And from Alky."

"You met Alky?"

"Everybody's met Alky. He's not shy."

"No," Mitch agreed. "He's not shy. I think he's going to be a good deputy."

"I'm sure he will," Jewel said. "But we're getting away from the subject I came here to talk about."

"What was that?"

"About how I had to find everything out from other people. I thought we were friends, Mitch."

The sound of his name sent a chill up Mitch's spine. He couldn't remember a woman who'd called him by his first name before, except for his mother. And Jewel definitely wasn't his mother.

She'd said they were friends. He'd been thinking along the same lines, but he wouldn't have gone so far as to put his thoughts into words. And now he didn't know how to respond to Jewel.

"Well?" she said, standing in front of his desk and glaring at him, her hands on her hips. "Are we friends or not?"

"I reckon we are."

"All right, then." Jewel relaxed slightly. "Why didn't you tell me the news?"

"I was busy. And then I didn't see you."

"You didn't look for me. I was at the Reverend Davis's services, looking things over, just the way you asked me to."

"Why don't you sit down," Mitch said. "You look uncomfortable standing there."

"I'm not uncomfortable. Are you uncomfortable?"

"Maybe." Mitch stood up and pulled the only other chair in the office over beside his desk. "Here. Sit down and help me out."

"Help you out? How?"

Mitch told her his trouble, how he wanted to organize his thoughts but things were so complicated he didn't even know what to start writing.

"So you aren't just trying to get me to keep quiet?" Jewel said. "You really do want me to help you?"

"I really do."

"Well, in that case, I'll sit down."

Mitch held the chair until she was seated. He didn't have any real idea about how to deal with women. Drunks and brawlers he could handle, but women were another story. He went back behind his desk and showed her the blank paper.

"That's how far I've got."

Jewel leaned toward him to look at the paper. Mitch handed it to her, and when she saw that there was nothing on it she handed it back.

"I don't know what you're going to write anything down for anyway. Why bother?"

Mitch tried to ignore the smell of her perfume and the way she made him feel. He asked what she meant.

"It seems to me that everything's been taken care of. You told me yourself that Gabriel was the man you'd been looking for."

"But I'm not sure. How can I be sure?"

"Maybe you can't. But think about it. How long had Gabriel been in town?"

"A day or so, at least. He'd been in the Bad Dog and caused a little trouble there."

Mitch went on to tell her what he'd heard from Collins.

"You see?" Jewel said. "He hated women. Two of them were killed, one of them that very night. But nobody died the next night. Why? Because you had Gabriel in jail. And no one was killed last night, either, because Gabriel was dead. Put that together with all those reasons you went riding after him, and you have to be sure that Gabriel was the man you wanted."

"It sure sounds like it when you explain it," Mitch admitted. "But it makes me wonder about something else, about who burned down Davis's tent. Now that I think about it, it could've been Gabriel. He was there making trouble after it happened, so maybe he's the one who burned it."

"That makes sense," Jewel said. "And him

being the killer makes a lot more sense than suspecting any of the other people I was watching at that meeting last night," Jewel said. "George Kelley, Bill Carson, John O'Connor, Ellie West. Could any of them really have killed those women?"

"You're leaving Davis off the list," Mitch reminded her.

"He doesn't make any more sense than any of the others."

She had a point, Mitch thought. John O'Connor had puked when he saw one of the bodies. That didn't sound much like the reaction of a killer to Mitch.

Kelley was a banker, and while Mitch knew that bankers could be just as human as anyone else, Kelley seemed entirely too respectable to sully his hands with murder, no matter how much a preacher might get him stirred up. Mitch figured that Kelley would be more likely to buy the whorehouse and shut down the whole place rather than resort to killing someone.

As for Bill Carson, he had a sickly wife who kept pretty much to herself but who would surely know if her husband had been slipping away at night to kill whores. And while Mitch had never met her, he'd heard she was the kind who wouldn't sit still for any slipping around of any kind.

Ellie West was a different story. She didn't have any ties to anyone, but while she was strong enough to have killed the women, she didn't seem to have the necessary hate inside her. Most of the whores, not being the kind of women who spent a lot of time cooking their own meals, ate at the Eat Here, and Ellie seemed to get along with them just fine.

That just left the Reverend Deuce Davis, and while Mitch wasn't ready to excuse him entirely, he didn't have any evidence that Davis had done a single thing other than preach some sermons that were calculated to cause trouble. As far as Mitch knew, there wasn't any law against that.

All right, then. Say Gabriel had a hatred of whores and preachers, so he killed the one and burned out the other. Say he went blank now and then and didn't know what he was doing, maybe because he was drunk, maybe because he was just crazy. Say he had an idea that he was crazy and that's why he showed Mitch the knife. It all hung together when you thought about it like that.

In fact, it all hung together so well that it worried Mitch. He felt as if there was still something he was missing, something that he'd seen or heard or should have noticed. And whatever that was, it would have given him a different answer.

"There's just one problem," he told Jewel, though there was more than one.

"Well, you'd better tell me what it is," she said. "I can't see it at all."

"There's a pretty good size loose end," Mitch said. "A question that we still haven't answered."

"What would that be?"

"If Gabriel killed the whores and burned the church, then who killed Gabriel?"

Jewel sighed. "I was afraid you were going to ask me that. I don't have an answer. I just have another question."

"That's what we need, all right. Another question. Let's have it."

"It's not just who killed him," Jewel said. "It's why."

121

"That's right. And there's something else you don't know, because I haven't told anybody."

"Keeping secrets again?"

"But not from you. I'm about to tell you what happened. Whoever shot Gabriel took a shot at me, too."

Mitch went on to tell her about the hour he'd spent behind the rock after getting his boot heel shot off.

"But how do you know it was the same person who killed Gabriel?" Jewel asked when he was finished.

"On the way back to town yesterday, Alky and I rode off the trail and checked for tracks. The same horse had been in both places. There weren't any other tracks. It was the same person, all right."

"So we've solved one mystery, but it's just left us with another one."

"That's the way it looks to me," Mitch said.

When Jewel left Mitch's office to go to have lunch with her father, they hadn't reached any further conclusions. Mitch rolled a cigarette and was having a smoke when Alky came in.

"That food at the Eat Here ain't bad," Alky said. "I might get to likin' this job all right, long's I don't have to go crawlin' on top of the bank ever' night."

"I can't make you any promises," Mitch said. "Have you checked on the prisoners this morning?"

"What d'you mean? Didn't I sleep in there with 'em last night? 'Course, I checked on 'em. They're all still right where we left 'em. Only difference is they're all awake and hungry now."

Mitch opened a desk drawer and got out the

keys. He tossed them to Alky and said, "You can let everybody out except Bowman. I don't think another day'll hurt him."

Alky grinned, showing crooked yellow teeth behind his whiskers. " 'Nother year or so wouldn't hurt that son of a bitch. You gonna give 'em back their weapons?"

They had searched the three men carefully, Mitch having learned a lesson from his experience with Gabriel. But the three most recent prisoners hadn't been carrying anything aside from their handguns, with the exception of Haskins, who'd had his Barlow knife. And in Haskins's hands it wasn't much of a weapon.

"We'll keep the weapons for a while," Mitch said. "You can tell them they can have them back if they attend the Reverend Davis's Sunday services."

Alky gave him a quizzical look. "You goin'?"

"I don't think so. Maybe I'll have a little talk with him later today, though."

"Get you some private preachin'?"

"Something like that," Mitch said.

It was around one o'clock in the afternoon when Davis finished his sermon, which he had preached in the Bad Dog Saloon, Red Collins having offered the premises since Davis was out of a tent and because the Bad Dog never did any business on Sunday mornings anyhow. Everyone was generally too hungover from the night before, so Collins gave everyone the morning off. He didn't even ask Davis for a cut of the offering.

Mitch came into the saloon just as the last of the crowd was straggling out. He saw Haskins and his other former prisoner, both of them still a little red-eyed and bleary. He told them to go by his office and have Alky give them their pistols back.

Bill Carson was there as well, and this time his wife was with him, clinging to his arm and looking sickly as ever, but feeling able to get out of the house during the daylight hours. She spoke softly to Mitch, who touched the brim of his hat and wished her a good day.

Then he made his way toward Davis, who was standing near the back of the big room, near the stage where every now and then one of Collins's girls would try to entertain the crowd by singing, usually with a notable lack of success, singing not being the talent for which Collins hired the women who worked for him. Mitch figured that Davis had used the stage as his pulpit and had most likely been far more entertaining than anyone Collins had ever put up there.

"Have you found out who burned my tent?" Davis asked when Mitch approached.

"I think so," Mitch said. "I think it was Gabriel, and you won't have to worry about him anymore."

"Don't feel bad about him. He tried to shoot me and everyone at the service that night. He would have if you hadn't showed up."

"He didn't like preachers," Mitch said. "And he didn't like women. I think he was taking it out on the town. But there's still something that bothers me."

"If it's the state of your immortal soul, there might be something I can do for you. Otherwise, I'm not sure that I can help."

"Maybe you can. What I'm trying to figure out is who killed Gabriel."

"You mean it wasn't you? That's the gossip around town."

"No," Mitch said, thinking that preachers should know better than to listen to gossip. "It wasn't me."

"And you think I might know who did it?"

"In a way," Mitch told him. "You see, I was thinking it might have been you."

Chapter Fifteen

Davis looked a little taken aback. "You know better than that, Sheriff. What are you trying to pull here?"

"Not a thing," Mitch told him. "It's just something I was wondering about."

No matter what he and Jewel had concluded about Gabriel, Mitch still wasn't satisfied. It was all too neat, and he didn't like that. Not when there was still that nagging itch at the back of his mind.

"Well, the answer is no," Davis said. "I didn't kill anybody." The preacher touched the scar on his face. "I might not look like much, but I'm a man of God. I don't take life. I show the way to eternal life through Jesus Christ."

"All the same, it strikes me that you might want to do something about the man who burned your tent."

"I know how to turn the other cheek," Davis

126

said. "And if a man compels me to go with him one mile, I'll go with him two."

"You didn't sound all that forgiving the other night when you were cutting those tent ropes."

"I'm a preacher," Davis said, "but I'm also just a man. There are times when my temper gets the better of my tongue and I fall back into using the kind of language I tried to put behind me many years ago. I've agonized about it many times, and I'm sure that I have God's forgiveness, just as Gabriel has mine."

"I guess we all need a little forgiveness now and then," Mitch said.

"Amen to that," Davis said. "Now, if you'll excuse me, I want to say a few words to Mr. Collins and thank him for the use of his place of business."

"I just have one other question," Mitch said.

Davis glanced over toward where Collins was standing, talking to a short man whose back was turned to Mitch. It looked a lot like Herman Tolliver to Mitch, who wondered where Spivey was.

Davis returned his glance to Mitch. "Well, ask your question," he said.

"What made you come to Paxton in the first place?"

"I thought it might be a place where souls needed saving. Boomtowns always are."

"And have you saved any souls?"

"That's another question, but I'll try to answer it. I baptized three men in the creek yesterday afternoon, and I'm going to baptize three more today. I expect they're waiting for me now."

"I'll let you go, then," Mitch said, and Davis walked over to have his word with Collins.

Mitch watched the two men for a minute as they talked, then left the saloon.

127

* * *

Fanny Belle's place was quiet on Sunday afternoons. Most of the men who visited there had taken their pleasure on Saturday night, and those who hadn't been at the saloon to hear were most likely working their claims or taking a day of rest.

"It's always nice to see you, Sheriff," Fanny Belle said by way of greeting when Mitch walked into the tent, "but it sure seems like you're dropping by a lot more regular lately. You got your eye on one of my girls?"

"That's not it," Mitch said. "They're all fine ladies, but I have something else on my mind."

"Well, you came to the right place to get it off. Want to have a little drink while you're doing it?"

Mitch turned down the offer, but Fanny Belle filled her glass. Mitch was beginning to think she had an endless capacity for liquor, as she never seemed to get the least bit addled in spite of her constant drinking.

"Here's to love," Fanny Belle said, lifting her glass before downing a hefty swallow of whiskey. "Now then, Sheriff, why don't you tell me what you had on your mind."

"It's about that fire," Mitch said.

"I've already told you about that. I didn't have anything to do with it, and neither did any of my girls. That preacher probably started it himself."

"It's not the fire, exactly," Mitch said. "And I don't think Davis started it. Looks like it was a man named Gabriel."

"The one you brought in yesterday across his own saddle?"

"That's the one."

Fanny Belle took a drink. "The talk is that you killed him. Is that right?"

"No. I'm trying to find out who did."

"It wasn't me. I hardly knew the fella."

Which might mean that she'd known him at least slightly. Mitch asked if that was the case.

Fanny Belle laughed, choked, took a drink. "That might be putting it too strong," she said when she was able. "Depends on what you mean by *knew*. But he was in here once or twice. I remember him."

That was what Mitch had been wondering about. He said, "How did he act? Any different from anybody else?"

"Hell, Sheriff, no two men act the same in a whorehouse. Some are shy, some are randy, and some are scared slap to death."

"Which one was Gabriel?"

Fanny Belle thought about it while she was finishing her drink. She poured another glass and said, "I don't remember every man who comes in here, Sheriff. I guess I remember him because he was one of the mannerly ones. Came in quiet, did his business without causing any trouble, and left."

That wasn't what Mitch had been hoping to hear. It didn't sound like the way a woman hater would behave.

"Which girl was he with?" he asked.

"Now, with all the men that come in here, how do you expect me to remember something like that?"

"You could try," Mitch said.

"What difference does it make? The man's dead, and my girls didn't kill him. They got better ways to spend their time."

"Let's just say you'd be doing me a favor if you could remember. In place of those free rides you offered me."

Fanny Belle drank nearly the full glass of whiskey before she spoke again. "You were probably thinking it was Star, but it wasn't. If I remember rightly, it was Rainbow."

Mitch touched the brim of his hat. "I thank you."

"You come back and see me again, Sheriff, you hear?" Fanny Belle called to him as he left, but Mitch was in too much of a hurry to reply.

Rainbow hadn't been awake for long when Mitch got to the shack where she and the other girls lived. She was sitting at a rickety table drinking coffee. Her hair was tousled, and she had a thin robe wrapped around her skinny body.

"I don't remember anybody named Gabriel," she said. "When a man comes to visit me, I don't ask for his name."

Mitch described Gabriel as best he could. "Do you remember anybody who looked like that?"

Rainbow shook her head. "I meet a lot of men in my line of work. I don't pay much attention to how they look."

Mitch knew that was probably true, but only in a limited sense. Paxton wasn't such a big place that there were that many men for Rainbow to see. Besides, lots of men had their special preferences, and they went back to the same woman again and again. He was pretty sure Rainbow knew who he was talking about. She was just being stubborn.

"Look," he said, "there's a possibility that he's the man who killed Star, but I don't know that for sure. I'm just trying to clear up a few things."

Rainbow took a sip from her coffee cup, avoiding Mitch's eyes. "I don't care about Star. She's dead. There's nothing I can do for her."

"Maybe you could. You might be able to help me be sure that Gabriel was really her killer."

"That wouldn't do Star any good."

"It might help her to rest easier. And it might do you some good too. So why don't you try to help the both of us."

"How can I do that?"

"Just tell me the truth. I want to know whether Gabriel was different from any of your usual customers. That's all."

Rainbow set the cup on the table and looked at Mitch. "Maybe I remember a little about him. If he's the one. They all look pretty much alike after a while."

"Tell me whatever you can."

"There's not much to tell. He was about like anybody else. Nothing special, or I'd remember him better."

Once again, that wasn't what Mitch had thought he might hear. He didn't quite know what to make of it.

"He wasn't rough? He didn't get mean?"

"Some men want to do that now and then, but I don't like it. And Fanny Belle won't put up with it."

Good for her, Mitch thought. He said, "So Gabriel didn't even try?"

"I told you: I'm not sure that's even the one I'm thinking of. But if it is, he was as nice as could be. Some men aren't. But he was."

Mitch knew there were men who liked to take advantage of whores because they were women with hardly any standing in society. If they were hurt, there was no one to protect them, and some men liked to hurt them. Mitch thought that Gabriel might have been like that, but apparently he wasn't.

That didn't fit the neat pattern that Mitch had been looking at earlier. If Gabriel hated all women, if he was a man who killed whores, then wouldn't he have acted differently when alone with one? Wouldn't he have tried to take advantage of her vulnerability and engage in some rough behavior as a prelude to murder?

It seemed to Mitch like that would be a good possibility, but it hadn't happened. So how did that affect the idea that Gabriel was a killer?

Mitch didn't know. "Have there been any other men lately who've tried getting rough with you or any of the others?"

"Not that I know of," Rainbow said. "I told you: Fanny Belle won't stand for it. If anybody tries something like that, she runs them off."

Mitch wondered what Fanny Belle would do if anyone didn't take to being run off. She didn't have a bouncer that Mitch knew of. Maybe she figured that was Mitch's job, but she hadn't had to call him for help yet. That probably meant that no one had gotten very violent, at least not since Mitch's arrival in Paxton.

Mitch didn't know what to make of it. The neat pattern was beginning to come apart. He thanked Rainbow for her help and left.

Alky was sitting in the office smoking his corncob pipe when Mitch got back. He wasn't sitting in Mitch's chair however, a fact that the sheriff appreciated. The room was filled with the smell of Alky's tobacco.

"Mighty quiet," the deputy said. "It always like this on a Sunday afternoon?"

"Most of the time," Mitch told him. "Enjoy it while you can."

Alky stood up. "Reckon I will. Want me to have a walk around town, see what's goin' on?"

Mitch didn't think anything was going on, but he wouldn't mind a few minutes alone to think about Gabriel.

"Go ahead. Come on back when you're done and we'll talk about tonight."

"What about tonight?"

"Sunday night's not as quiet as Sunday afternoon," Mitch said.

Alky scratched his whiskers. "All right. I'll be back in an hour or so."

Mitch sat down and watched Alky's back as the deputy went out the door. Maybe he should have talked things over with him, but Alky didn't seem particularly curious about Gabriel's murder. He probably didn't have any ideas to contribute.

For that matter, Mitch didn't have any ideas either. But what worried him even more was what was going to happen if he and Jewel were wrong about Gabriel.

If Gabriel hadn't been the killer, then someone else was likely going to die.

But no one had been killed for the last two nights. The town was quiet, sleeping on the side of the mountain on a Sunday afternoon as peacefully as if the two murders had never happened. That must mean that everything was all right again. Didn't it? Mitch wished he knew.

Chapter Sixteen

Sula Lee had never been too smart in school, not that there had been much of a school where Sula grew up. Just one room where all the kids went to learn to read and write and cipher as much as was possible for them with a teacher like Mr. Martin, who seemed a lot more interested in keeping order than in teaching anything.

Mr. Martin had been mean as hell, as Sula well remembered. He seemed to get a lot of pleasure from whipping anyone who so much as said a word during the lessons, and what he enjoyed even more was giving a good hiding to anybody who didn't perform up to his standards when it came time to recite.

Sula had received more than her share of whippings. For some reason or another, Mr. Martin seemed to like whipping her more than the others. Maybe it was because she had filled out earlier than any of the other girls. By the time she was twelve, she looked like a woman fully grown, and Mr. Martin had taken to having her stay after school for her whippings. "So I can pull up your dress and do an honest job of it" was the way he put it.

When her daddy found out about that, he went to the school one afternoon and had a few words with Mr. Martin. Or maybe he had more than words, since nobody ever saw Mr. Martin around town again.

"Good enough for the son of a bitch if he never comes back," Sula's father told her. "And as for you, you've had all the schooling you need. I never saw the need for sending a girl to school in the first place. It's like teaching a hog to read. Waste of time."

From that day on, Sula worked around the house instead of going to school, and it was her father who whipped her when she didn't do to suit him. She decided things weren't any better that way than they'd been at school, and she left as soon as she was able.

Not having any education or training, not knowing any kind of trade, and not having a husband, she drifted into her profession the way so many others did. It didn't take any training, and it was a way to make a few dollars without having to work very hard. All you had to do was what came naturally, and Sula found that she was good at that. It was the only thing she'd ever been good at before, and she enjoyed the work, even if nobody respected her for doing it. It sure beat getting a whipping.

Which was why she never let anyone get away with something like that with her on the job. There were other girls who didn't seem to mind, and there were even a few who seemed to like it. Sula thought that was pretty damned strange, but she didn't care much. If they liked it, that was fine with her, just as long as no one asked her to take part.

"That's exactly the way I feel, too," Rainbow said when she and Sula talked it over. "I wonder why the sheriff wanted to know if that Gabriel fella was that way?"

Sula shrugged. "I'm just glad he's dead and we don't have to worry about him anymore."

"You really think he was the one that killed Star?"

"That's what people are saying. I guess it must be so."

Rainbow yawned, losing interest in the conversation. She closed her mouth and said, "Have you been to hear that preacher yet?"

"No. Have you?"

"Sure. It was a real good sermon, too. You should go tonight. There won't be much going on around here."

"I think I will," Sula said.

The services were held outside that evening. The Reverend Davis promised that a new tent was on the way, and he thanked everyone for their generous offerings that had made it possible. Sula reminded herself to give something when the plate came around.

She enjoyed the singing and the preaching more than she'd thought she would. It reminded her in a way of how things had been when she was a little girl and her mother would take her to church now and then. That was before her mother had died and her father had run off the schoolteacher. She hadn't been to church since.

Sula hummed one of the hymns to herself as she walked back to Fanny Belle's. It was one she remembered from a long time ago. She'd left the service before the final altar call, and everyone else was still there, waiting for the benediction. It was dark in the street, but it was a nice night, and Sula looked up at all the stars. It seemed to her there were more of them than there'd been when she was a girl, but maybe it had something to do with being up on the side of a mountain.

"Hey, girlie," a voice said from an alley. "How 'bout a little fun."

Sula started at the sound. She might not have done well in school, but she wasn't stupid. She knew what had happened to Star, and she wasn't going to let it happen to her. She didn't even give the alley a second glance. She started to run.

But she didn't get far. Someone jumped on her back and threw her to the ground. She wanted to scream, but she couldn't get a breath because the person on her back had knocked the air from her lungs and was pressing her face into the street. When she tried to cry out, all she got was a mouthful of dirt.

She tried to turn her head to the side, and just as she did her head was jerked up. She might have screamed then, but a forearm across her windpipe cut off the air, and she thought for a second that her neck was going to snap.

It didn't, but it felt as if it had. Then she was jerked to her feet and dragged backward. She still couldn't get any air.

She tried struggling and kicking, but it did no good. Whoever had her was too strong for her, and she was rapidly losing consciousness because she couldn't breathe.

She thought this was worse than the whippings her father had given her, worse than the ones she'd gotten from Mr. Martin. She'd finally escaped those, but this time, she thought, there would be no getting away.

She was right about that, and almost the last thing she felt was when the forearm across her neck relaxed just the slightest bit and a tiny stream of air flowed into her burning lungs.

But then the sharp, stinging edge of the knife was drawn across her neck; as the soft skin parted, all the air went out of her, and there was no getting it back.

There was a lot of blood, and Sula's hands brushed at it weakly as if trying to keep it off her dress, but she was beyond caring about that.

She was beyond caring about anything at all.

Chapter Seventeen

This time the body was found almost immediately after the murder, by J. Paxton Reid himself. And by Jewel, who was walking back from Davis's evening service with him when he thought he heard something in the alley they were passing.

"So I told her to stay where she was while I had a look," he told Mitch. "When I saw what was back there, I was glad she wasn't with me."

They were standing over the body of Sula Lee. Alky was with them, holding a lantern that made shadows jump off the walls of the buildings and the white tents. Jewel had been sent to find Evan Riley. She was furious because her father wouldn't let her see what was going on, but she had gone to look for Riley anyhow.

Standing out in the street, all bunched together, were thirty or so of the others who'd been at the preaching. Mitch had warned them to stay there, though all of them were eager for a sight of the latest carnage.

"Buncha damn vultures," Alky said. "You'd think goin' to church woulda taught 'em something."

"You know who it is?" Reid asked Mitch.

"No, but I'm guessing she's one of the whores from Fanny Belle's or the Bad Dog. You didn't see anybody when you came back here?"

"There was somebody, I think. I heard a noise. But if anybody was here, he ran away when I walked in the alley. I guess I could have chased him, but I couldn't have caught him. Besides, I guess you could say I was a little too dazed to do anything. I never saw anything like this, not close up, not just after it happened, anyhow."

There was the smell of blood and butchery in the alley. Sula wasn't pretty, though she once had been. Like the others who'd been killed, she'd been mutilated with a knife. Mitch hadn't looked yet, but he wondered if she had both her ears.

He bent down and brushed Sula's hair back from the right side of her face. The ear was missing. Mitch stood up.

"What did Davis preach about this evening?" he asked "Whores again?"

"No," Reid said. "He didn't even mention that topic. He's on to drinking now. It's like he's against every pleasure the men in this town have. If he keeps it up, he won't have anybody to listen to him. They'll all turn against him."

Mitch was thinking about that when Evan Riley showed up, followed closely by Jewel Reid.

"I thought I told you not to come back here," Reid said.

"If I can live in this town, I can see what happens here," Jewel said. She looked down at Sula's body. "My God."

"Looks like we'll be needing another casket," Evan Riley said. "This one's as bad as the others."

"I'm just as glad I wasn't around to see 'em, then," Alky said. "I guess this means that Gabriel fella wasn't the guilty party."

"It looks that way," Mitch agreed.

He'd been uneasy about the possibility of Gabriel's guilt all along, but now that he was proved right, he didn't feel particularly happy about it. In fact, he felt pretty damned bad, considering the result.

"We can't have this kind of thing in Paxton," Reid said to Mitch. "You have to put a stop to it."

"I've been trying," Mitch told him. "For a while there it looked like things were going to be all right."

"Well, they aren't," Reid said. "And you'd damn well better do something about it."

"If you don't like the way I'm doing the job," Mitch said, "you can have my resignation right now."

That stopped Reid for a second. But he recovered quickly. "It's not as easy to quit as all that, Frye. I know you're trying your best. And I know you'll get to the bottom of things sooner or later."

"I sure hope it's sooner," Alky said. "I don't think I can stand too much of this."

"You're not the only one," Mitch said.

After the body had been taken care of, Mitch went and got Fanny Belle, who was able to identify Sula Lee as one of her girls. She was even more upset than Reid and even more insistent that Mitch do something.

He assured her that he would, though he had no idea what he was going to do or how he was going to do it. He sent Alky out to patrol, and for the rest of the night he sat in his office, rolled cigarettes, smoked them, and thought about the women who'd been killed. He also thought about the Reverend Davis and the sermons he'd preached.

Somewhere around two or three o'clock, an idea occurred to him. He finally knew what had been bothering him about Gabriel, and he hated himself for not having thought of it earlier. But it would have required him to ask a question that most people in Paxton just didn't ask. Mitch hadn't asked it of Alky either, though as sheriff he certainly had a right to do it, especially since he'd made Alky his deputy.

Not having asked was a result of his having been a lawman only a short time, like overlooking Gabriel's knife. He was going to have to start thinking in a different kind of way now, one that he wasn't used to. He hoped he was able to do it before anybody else got killed because of his mistakes.

He thought for a minute about going and rousting Sam Neely out of bed, but he thought better of it. He'd just make Sam angry, and what he wanted to do could wait until morning. That night's killing had already been done.

Mitch slept only a couple of hours, and then he was up and on the way to Neely's place. Sam was already at work, feeding the animals he boarded.

"You're up mighty early, Sheriff," he said when Mitch walked in. "You must need something."

The place was full of the smells of smoke and horses and grain, all good smells that made Mitch want to take a deep breath and forget why he was there. He took the breath, but he couldn't forget.

"You're right," he told Sam. "I do need something. I need to look through those saddlebags I brought in the other day."

"You mean the dead man's. I thought you went through those already."

"I didn't do a very good job," Mitch said.

That was another one of his mistakes, which like the others came from inexperience. He'd checked to see if the saddlebags held anything valuable, which they hadn't, but he'd overlooked other things that might have been even more important.

And it wasn't as if Gabriel hadn't been teasing him with the answer. Mitch had thought it was the knife that mattered, but that hadn't been it at all, not if Mitch was right this time. He'd have to look in the saddlebags to be sure, and even then he might not find what he was looking for.

"I'll get 'em for you," Neely said, and went off to get the saddlebags. He came back in a minute and said, "Where do you want 'em?"

"I'll take them back to my office," Mitch said as Neely handed them to him. "Thanks for your trouble."

"If all my jobs were that easy, I wouldn't have any complaints," Neely said.

Mitch didn't reply. He was already on his way out the wide double door.

When Alky came in, Mitch had the contents of the saddlebags spread out on his desk.

"Looks like you're busy," Alky said. "But I got to ask you a question anyhow."

Mitch looked up at him. "Ask."

"What about that Injun-hater we got locked up? Don't you think it's time we turned him loose?"

"We might as well. You can let him out. Tell him

that if he stays out of trouble for a week, he can have his pistol back. After you turn him out, come back here. You can go on a little visit with me."

"All right. You think he's learned his lesson?"

"I doubt it. Men like that don't ever learn much."

"You're prob'ly right. We'll have him locked up again inside that week you're givin' him."

Mitch said that he wouldn't be surprised.

Alky started to leave, then turned back. "What's all that stuff, anyhow?"

"It's from Gabriel's saddlebags. I was looking to see if there was anything in there that might answer a question I had."

"What was it you were lookin' for?"

"A letter, a receipt, anything like that."

Alky looked at the small stack of papers that was on the desk. "Looks like you found what you wanted, then."

"That's right."

"What did it tell you?"

"Gabriel's last name," Mitch said.

Chapter Eighteen

Jewel came in just as Mitch and Alky were about to leave.

"You weren't at breakfast again," she said to Mitch. "Why does that make me think you're keeping secrets?"

"I forgot about breakfast," he said, realizing that even though he had, he wasn't at all hungry. "I was thinking of something else."

Jewel looked at the desk. "Does it have anything to do with that mess there?"

Mitch told her that it did, and he explained what he'd found.

"You mean that Gabriel is Davis's brother?" she said when he'd finished.

"I don't know that for sure. But he told me his brother was a preacher. He said he got fed up with the way their mother was always comparing them. And he had a receipt in there with the name Gabriel Davis on it. What does that sound like to you?"

"They weren't anything alike," Jewel said.

"Brothers don't always get along," Alky said. "And they don't always travel down the same road."

"That's right enough," Jewel said. "And it might explain why Gabriel shot up the meeting. It was his way of getting back at his brother."

"It might even tell us the answer to another question," Mitch said.

"What's that?"

"We might know who tried to burn the tent."

"We might," Jewel said. "But all your answers just seem to bring up more questions."

"I'm way ahead of you," Mitch said. "Here's the main one: Why didn't Davis tell us that Gabriel was his brother in the first place?"

"And while you're thinking about that," Jewel said, "you can wonder about what Davis's first name is. Deuce is just a nickname, remember. Do you think maybe he might have an angel's name, too?"

"I don't know too many angels' names," Mitch said. "But we can ask."

"Now, that's the best idea you've had in a while," Jewel said. "Let's go."

"I think you'd better stay here," Mitch told her.

"I'm getting a little fed up with people telling me that. It seems like that's all I've heard the last few days."

Mitch looked at Alky, who was no help. He just shrugged and looked the other way. So Mitch said, "All right. Let's go."

Mitch had hoped to find Davis in his room, but the hotel clerk told them that the new tent had arrived and Davis had gone to supervise its raising.

When Mitch, Jewel, and Alky arrived on the scene, the tent was still in the back of a wagon. Davis had a crew of men clearing the ground, and the smoky smell of dead ashes filled the air. Mitch saw Tolliver, Spivey, and even Haskins among the crew that was shoveling ashes into large piles to be carried away later.

Mitch walked over to Davis and said, "Is there somewhere we can go and have a talk?"

"I'm sure you and your friends are interesting conversationalists," Davis said, "but I have work to do here, as you can see. Can't we have our talk some other time?"

"I'm afraid not," Mitch said. "It's about your brother."

Davis flinched only slightly. If Mitch hadn't been looking for it, he might not even have noticed.

"Brother?" Davis said. "I don't have any brother."

"Not anymore you don't," Alky said, raising his voice a little. "That's because somebody killed him yesterday."

Davis turned away. "I don't know what you're talking about, and neither do you. And I don't have time for listening. I have the Lord's work to do here."

"Hang on a minute," Mitch said as he pulled the receipt from his shirt pocket. "It says here that the man who was killed was named Gabriel Davis. That might not prove anything, but it's mighty suspicious, especially considering that he told me his brother was a preacher. He didn't like his brother much, either. He might do something mean to him, like burn his tent or shoot up his congregation."

"It won't be hard to find out the truth," Jewel said. "You might as well tell us now and save everyone some trouble."

"Yeah, and you might as well tell us what your first name is, too," Alky said. "It wouldn't be Michael, now, would it?"

Davis's eyes narrowed just slightly, and Mitch knew that Alky had made a lucky guess. Or maybe it was more than a guess, since Alky said, "Gabriel and Michael. The two chief angels. I'm glad to see I got a little use from those Sunday school lessons my ma made me sit through all those years ago. Ma'd be downright proud of me."

Davis looked around and saw that some of the cleaning crew were watching them with open curiosity. He said, "All right. I'll talk to you. Let's move away from here so we won't have too many listeners."

Mitch resisted the urge to tell him that he'd suggested that earlier, and they walked over to the wagon where the tent was waiting.

"It's true that Gabriel was my brother," Davis said when they were out of earshot of the workers. "But we didn't get along. He was different from me. Or at least he was different from the way I am now. I have to admit that I was much like him when I was younger, but I changed my ways, and he never could accept it. He thought I was just trying some new scheme to make money." Davis's mangled hand went to the scar on his face. "Gabriel couldn't seem to understand that I had more than a sufficient reason to begin leading a new life."

"Your ma musta been proud of you, too," Alky said.

"That was another problem for Gabriel," Davis said. "Our mother could never quit harping on how he should change his ways and be more like me. Of course, that just made him more intent on being different."

"Did he follow you here to make trouble?" Mitch asked.

Davis shrugged. "That's hard to say. We were never close, and we didn't keep up with each other. We certainly never had much affection for each other, and we had a lot less after my life changed. We've run into each other once or twice in the past. When we did, he always tried to stir things up, to cause as much trouble for me as he could. But he never went so far as to burn the tent or shoot up the congregation. I don't know what got into him."

"Whiskey," Mitch said. "Did you know he had times when he couldn't remember what he'd done?"

"We weren't exactly on the best of terms," Davis said. "I didn't know about that, but I knew he drank."

"I thought at first he might be killing those women, and then forgetting he'd done it," Mitch said. "He couldn't remember shooting up your crowd. And he didn't say a thing about burning the tent. He probably didn't recall that, either."

"I've heard such things can happen," Davis said. "But I'm not sure it was true in Gabriel's case. I think it could be just a way he had of excusing his transgressions."

"So maybe you decided to put a stop to those transgressions, as you call 'em," Alky said. "Is that it?"

Davis straightened his shoulders. "I don't believe in violence and retaliation. 'Vengeance is mine, saith the Lord.'"

"It wasn't the Lord that rode down the mountain and killed your brother," Mitch said. "It was somebody purely human."

"It might have been that Gabriel brought it on

himself," Davis said. "He could have insulted someone or gotten into a fight."

Mitch shook his head. "He didn't have the time. He went from the jail to the livery, and from there he went right on out of town. Whoever killed him, it wasn't anybody that he'd run into that morning."

"It could have been someone he met on the road," Davis suggested. "A robbery, or an argument."

"I'm the one he met on the road," Alky said. "Or he would've if somebody hadn't shot him. We didn't argue, and I didn't shoot him. Besides, the sheriff says that tracks of his killer led back up the mountain."

"That's all true," Mitch said. "So where does that leave us?"

"It doesn't leave me anywhere except right here," Davis said. "I'm sorry my brother's dead, but I don't plan to do any grieving for him. He wouldn't have expected it, considering the way he felt about me."

"Don't you even want to preach his funeral?" Jewel asked. "It seems like the least you could do for your bother."

"I might do that," Davis told her, and Mitch thought the preacher got entirely too much satisfaction out of saying it. It was almost as if he was glad his brother was dead.

Still, after talking to Davis, Mitch didn't think he was the killer. At least he was honest about the way he and his brother felt about each other. Besides, Mitch had seen Davis talking to someone when he rode out after Gabriel, and Davis probably wasn't a good enough rider to have gotten ahead of Mitch while he was delayed by Reid. It was more likely that Gabriel had been killed by someone who'd left town ahead of Mitch.

But that someone could have been sent by Davis.

"Did you think your brother was killing those women?" he asked.

"What would I care about that? They were only harlots."

Jewel took a step toward Davis, and for a second Mitch thought she might jump on him and try to whip him. She stopped short and glared at him instead.

"You might be a preacher," she said, "but you don't know much about compassion and understanding."

"Those women aren't deserving of compassion," Davis said. "What they do is contrary to the will of God."

"It must be nice to be so certain that you have all the answers," Jewel said. "And to know that you're always in the right."

"God's word never fails."

Jewel's face got red. She took a deep breath, turned, and walked away.

Mitch said, "I take it you wouldn't kill your brother to keep him from murdering those whores, then."

"Not for that, or for any other reason. Now, if you'll leave me be, I'll see about getting back to work."

Mitch hadn't noticed Davis doing any of the actual labor, but he didn't say so. He watched as the preacher walked back over to where the others were working.

"I can't stand self-righteous people like that," Jewel said when Davis was gone. "They think they know the only right way, and they want to force everyone else to be like them."

"Doesn't seem to miss his brother all that much, either," Alky added.

"That doesn't make him a killer," Mitch told them.

"Maybe not," Jewel said. "But it doesn't make him much of a human being, either." She looked over at Davis with distaste. "Well, what do we do next? Start all over?"

"I don't think so," Mitch said. "We're on the right track here. There's something that I'm overlooking, but I just can't quite put my finger on it."

"Something to do with Davis?" Jewel asked.

"I'm sure of it. I just can't make it come clear."

"One thing I'll have to give that preacher credit for," Alky said. "He must preach a powerful sermon to have so many folks working for him while he does the supervisin'."

"Even those two men you had to put in jail, Mitch," Jewel said. "They said some awful things, but there they are, working for the Lord."

"I doubt it's changed their feelings about me," Mitch said. "Somehow it usually turns out to be all right to hate Indians, no matter how much religion you have."

"And harlots," Jewel added. "Don't forget the harlots."

"Don't worry," Mitch said. "I won't."

As they started back toward town, Davis called out to them. "If you'd like to lend a hand in the Lord's work, we'd appreciate the help."

"We have our own work to do," Jewel told him.

"But is it Godly work?"

"It's close enough to it for me," Alky said.

"He cares more about getting that tent up for tonight's service than he does about whoever killed those women," Jewel said. "He must have a heart as hard as this mountain we're on."

"Lots of people care more about themselves

than about what happens to somebody else," Alky said. "I've noticed that all over."

"You're not like that," she said. "Neither is Mitch."

"When you've been kicked around a little, you can appreciate how bad it feels," Alky said. "So you try to help out if you can."

"Sort of makes you wonder who's the better Christian, doesn't it?" Jewel said.

Alky smiled. "I didn't know it was a contest."

"You're right," Jewel said. "I don't suppose it is."

Chapter Nineteen

They were almost to the office when they met J. Paxton Reid, who wanted to know where Jewel had been.

"There's work at my office," he said, "and you should be there to do it, not hanging around with—"

He stopped and looked at Mitch and Alky.

"Better watch what you call us," Alky cautioned him. "Your daughter's on a real tear about the way people act toward other folks."

"No offense," Reid said. "I didn't mean that the way it sounded."

Mitch figured Reid had meant it exactly the way it sounded, all right, but he didn't call him on it. He was too busy worrying about other things.

"Maybe it would do us all good to go to those services tonight," he said.

"You don't really mean that, do you?" Jewel said. "Not after the way Davis talked just now."

"I really mean it," Mitch assured her. "Those services are the key to the whole thing, one way or the other. I can feel it."

"Well, I hope you're right about that," Reid said. "I don't want any more killing in this town."

"See?" Alky said to Jewel. "Ever'body has a good side if you just give 'em a chance."

"Sometimes you have to look too hard," Jewel said, walking away from them.

"Who put a burr under her saddle?" Reid asked of no one in particular.

It was Alky who answered. "That preacher, for one. And I don't think she took too well to what you said, either."

"I apologized for that," Reid said, though he didn't look contrite.

"It doesn't matter," Mitch said.

Reid didn't agree. "If it upset Jewel, it matters. Maybe you're right. Maybe we'll get some good out of those services tonight."

"We'll see," Mitch said.

But it wasn't good he was really looking for. It was answers.

The afternoon was quiet. Mitch and Alky had to subdue a drunk who decided that the bartender at the Bad Dog was trying to poison him. Alky convinced the man that while the whiskey wasn't exactly the best in the world, it wasn't poisonous, either.

"Might be in the long run," Mitch said. "If he drinks enough of it."

They had put the man in the jail, and the smell of liquor filled the place.

"I don't think you could convince him to quit it," Alky said. "I don't even think that preacher could. I expect he likes the stuff too much to do that."

"You could be right," Mitch agreed. "We'll let him sleep it off and turn him loose in the morning. In the meantime, you can go on patrol this evening while I go to hear the preaching."

"You think it'll be any help?"

"You never can tell," Mitch said.

The Reverend Davis's new tent wasn't exactly new, and the smell of ashes was still powerful, overwhelming the smell of the canvas. Mitch and Jewel sat with Reid in the back row, and Mitch scanned the crowd. Red Collins wasn't there, and no wonder. What with Davis railing against liquor now, the saloon owner wasn't likely to appreciate anything the preacher said. But Mitch saw Haskins, Neely, O'Connor, Kelley, and Bill Carson without his wife. Right down on the front row were Tolliver and Spivey. Mitch wondered if they'd be taking up the offering.

There was some singing, a scripture or two, and some more singing, but Mitch wasn't paying much attention. He was wondering what didn't seem right about the whole thing.

And then, after a while, he thought he knew. Everything that had been all jumbled around in his head just seemed to rearrange itself into a pattern that made sense.

If you were going to cause trouble in a town by killing a few of its citizens, what would be the best disguise you could assume?

Being a preacher might be the best, but Mitch had already decided that Davis was just what he appeared to be: a self-righteous evangelist who might know how to hold a grudge but who wouldn't actually kill anyone.

So the next best thing might be to become so close to the preacher that people thought you were just as pious as he was. You might have a bad reputation, but you could appear to have changed your life completely. Davis claimed to have done it in reality, but others could do it by pretense.

And who'd done that? Tolliver and Spivey, that's who. They'd gone from being Indian-hating troublemakers to Davis's right-hand men, and as Mitch had pointed out to Alky when they'd talked about releasing Bowman, that kind of change didn't usually occur. Mitch didn't deny that it was possible, but if it was, it was awfully rare. So rare, in fact, that Mitch had never seen it.

Mitch thought back over the events of the past few days, and he knew what had been bothering him all along. Tolliver and Spivey had said that Jewel was no better than a whore because of her association with Mitch. Obviously they didn't like whores very much, and probably not women in general. There was a connection right there.

And he hadn't searched them when he put them in jail. Either of them could have had a knife concealed in his boot.

The two of them had told him he'd be sorry for jailing them. He'd thought it was just an idle threat. But maybe it hadn't been. Maybe they'd really meant it and had decided to make him sorry by punishing him and the whole town.

Mitch thought about some other things that had happened. Who'd been standing next to Davis just before the preacher yelled out that the whores had burned his tent? Tolliver had, and he'd probably been the one to suggest it. Gabriel hadn't burned the tent, after all. It had been Tolliver and Spivey, who'd tried to blame Fanny Belle and her girls in order to cause even more trouble for Mitch and the whole town. Probably it had been Davis's sermons that had given them the idea of attacking the whores in the first place.

That left Gabriel's murder, which Mitch figured could be pinned on Spivey. When Mitch had ridden out of town, he'd seen Tolliver and Davis together, but Spivey hadn't been anywhere around. He and Tolliver might have decided that killing Gabriel would be a favor to Davis, or maybe they thought Gabriel knew something about their activities. They couldn't have known that even if Gabriel had seen anything happen late at night, he most likely wouldn't remember it. In fact, he hadn't reported anything to Mitch, who was sure that Gabriel would have told him had he known anything about the murders.

And on his way back to town, Spivey might have taken a shot at Mitch just for spite. He probably wouldn't have wanted to kill him, not yet, just have a little sport with him. Spivey and Tolliver were having too much fun to kill Mitch. They'd want to get the town a little more stirred up before they tried that.

Everything fit, Mitch decided, although he knew that he might be mistaken. After all, he'd been wrong about Gabriel. If he could find out where Spivey kept his horse, he'd know for sure. He could check the prints, and then there wouldn't be any doubt, one way or the other.

Mitch came out of his musing as Davis was reaching a high point of his sermon. He was saying that the only difference between a drunk and a lunatic was that a drunk could go to sleep and wake up halfway sane again. The only trouble was, according to Davis, the drunk was more likely to wake up in a hog wallow than a feather bed.

Mitch had some experience with being drunk, and as much as he hated to admit it, Davis was right about the last part.

But that didn't make any difference right now. Mitch had to find out about Spivey's horse. That wouldn't be easy. All he knew for sure was that the horse wasn't stabled at Neely's livery. There were any number of other places in town where a horse could be kept, and Spivey might have a mining claim somewhere on the mountain. His horse might be there.

Or he might have ridden it to the services. Mitch decided it might be a good idea to have a look around.

He stood up to leave, but Jewel tugged at his shirtsleeve. He bent down to hear what she had to say.

"Where are you going?" she whispered in his ear.

"There's something I have to check out."

"I'll come with you."

She started to rise, but Mitch put a hand on her arm and pushed her back down.

"This isn't important," he said. "I'll tell you about it later."

Jewel looked up at him. "You'd better."

Mitch nodded and turned to leave the tent. On his way out, he took one of the lanterns that Davis used to light the service. He'd need that to see the tracks of the horses out back in the little makeshift rope corral that had been set up for the convenience of people who rode to the services. If the horse Mitch was looking for happened to be there, it wouldn't even matter if it was Spivey's mount. Mitch could just wait for someone to come for it. But he was pretty sure that if the horse was there, it would belong to Spivey.

The horses were docile and didn't stir around much when Mitch started moving among them. He held the lantern close to the ground to see if any of the tracks matched those he'd seen near where Gabriel had been killed.

Besides having to contend with the dim light of the lantern, Mitch discovered that the ground was hard and the horses had trampled it so much that he had trouble distinguishing any of the prints. He was afraid he wasn't going to be able to distinguish one set of tracks from another. He could go around lifting up the horse's feet, but the horses might not want to cooperate with him.

He was about to give it up and leave when he thought he heard something behind him. The horses shifted nervously, and Mitch started to turn.

Sam Spivey stood there, holding his pistol. Spivey said, "Looking for something, you Indian son of a bitch?"

Chapter Twenty

Mitch completed his turn by bringing his arm around and flinging the lantern right at Spivey's nose, which was still slightly swollen from their previous encounter.

Spivey yelled, but he didn't drop the pistol. The lantern bounced off his head and fell to the ground. Coal oil splattered, the glass broke, and the flame ignited the coal oil. The fire sputtered in the trampled grass. It wouldn't burn for long, but it panicked the horses, all of which started whinnying and stamping and lunging against the ropes, which weren't going to hold up to much pressure.

Mitch dived behind one of the horses, pulling his own pistol as he fell. He rolled over, hoping for a clear shot at Spivey. The flickering flames showed him one of Spivey's legs between those of a plunging horse, and he snapped off a shot at Spivey's knee. The shot and the screams that followed were all it took to terrorize the horses completely.

Spivey crumpled, dropped his pistol, and fell into the flames. His clothing caught fire almost at once, and he thrashed from side to side. One of the horses stepped on him as it tried to escape the enclosure, and he screamed even more loudly.

Mitch stood up just as the horses broke through the ropes and escaped. They headed straight for the tent.

Davis's congregation had ample warning that something was going on, but none of them had left the tent yet. When they saw the horses coming for them, they poured out through the open sides and ran for the cover of the nearest buildings. The Reverend Davis was in the lead.

The horses crashed through the tent, destroying Davis's newly carpentered pulpit and splintering the makeshift benches. Some of them caught the guy ropes on the outside, and the tent began to fall. All the people and horses were gone before it collapsed completely, and the horses pounded away down the mountain.

Mitch was sorry about that. It was going to be quite an inconvenience for the people at the meeting to round them up. They probably wouldn't get it done for a day or so.

But at least Mitch had Spivey. He walked over to him and helped him roll over and over to put out the burning clothing. When Spivey was lying still, his clothes hardly smoldering, Mitch stood over him and said, "Was Tolliver in on it?"

Spivey didn't have to answer. Tolliver said from behind Mitch, "You're damn right I was, you chickenshit redskin."

When he turned this time, Mitch had his pistol ready, but he wasn't ready for what he saw. Tolliver was standing behind Jewel, and his pistol wasn't pointing at Mitch. It was held to the back of Jewel's head.

"I see you figured it out," Tolliver said. "And it looks like you shot Sam besides. Too damn bad for him. Too damn bad for you, too. This bitch of yours started all the trouble, and she's going to be the finish of it."

"You and Spivey started it," Mitch said. "She doesn't have a thing to do with it."

"I guess we'll see about that," Tolliver said. "You might get me, but by then she'll be dead."

"I wouldn't count on that if I was you," Alky said, walking out of the darkness.

Tolliver whirled and shot him, but to do so he had to release his hold on Jewel, who shoved him to the side as hard as she could.

He turned back to fire at her, but Mitch shot him in the bridge of his nose. Tolliver's head snapped back, and then his knees buckled. He fell and lay still.

Mitch walked over to him and kicked the gun from his limp fingers. Then he went to check Spivey. Spivey had been shot, burned, and stepped on by a horse, but Mitch had to give the son of a bitch credit. He was game to the end. He'd crawled or wriggled over to where his pistol lay and picked it up. He was pointing it unsteadily at Mitch and trying to pull the trigger.

Mitch didn't hesitate. He shot him in the right eye. Spivey's head slammed back into the hard ground. His left foot kicked twice, as if he were trying to shake something off his boot, and then the pistol dropped from his limp fingers.

Mitch turned away and went to where Alky was being helped into a sitting position by Jewel. He had his right hand pressed on his left shoulder, and blood was leaking between his fingers and staining his shirt.

"You never said nothin' about gettin' shot bein' part of the job," Alky said.

"I must've forgotten that part," Mitch said. "Are you going to be all right?"

"I reckon so. I lost more blood than this to some mosquitoes I run into down in Texas one time."

"How about you?" Mitch asked Jewel.

"I'm fine. But I'm not so sure about my father."

"Where is he?"

Jewel pointed to the fallen tent. "Back there. That man hit him in the head with his gun."

"I'll see about him," Mitch said. "You stay here with Alky."

"You go ahead," Alky told her. "I can take care of myself. Besides, looks like plenty of help's comin' now that there's no trouble."

He was right. People were leaving the shelter of the buildings and coming out to see what had happened.

Jewel stood up, and she and Mitch went to look for Reid. They found him near the edge of the tent, lying still on the ground. At first Mitch was afraid he'd been trampled by the horses, but then he started groaning. Mitch knelt down and looked him over.

"I think he's okay," he said. "I'll help him get up."

He put his hands under Reid's armpits and helped him sit up. Reid put a hand to the back of his head and said, "What the hell happened?"

"Somebody hit you," Jewel said.

"Why?"

"He was after your daughter," Mitch told him. "But don't worry. She's fine now."

"She'd damn well better be. What was going on here, anyhow?"

"I'm not sure," Jewel said. "But I think Mr. Frye just took care of the men who killed those women."

"Is that right, Frye?"

"That's right. They won't be killing anybody else."

"Well, then, you were right. We got some good out of the services tonight after all. Looks like those horses made a mess of the preacher's tent, though."

"The town can't be responsible for that," Mitch said.

He helped Reid to his feet. Reid said, "That preacher might have a different idea. Here he comes."

"You can deal with him," Mitch said. "You're the mayor."

"Where are you going?" Reid asked.

"To see about my deputy."

Later, he would check Tolliver and Spivey's pockets to see which one of them had kept the ears.

"I'll help you," Jewel said, and they left Reid standing there, gently touching the tender spot on his head.

TROUBLE MAN

ED GORMAN

Ray Coyle used to be a gunfighter. And when he gets word his boy has been killed in a gunfight in Coopersville, he has to go there—to bring the body home. But when the old gunfighter steps off the train, he brings his gun with him, along with something else . . . trouble.

___4440-4 $4.99 US/$5.99 CAN

Dorchester Publishing Co., Inc.
P.O. Box 6640
Wayne, PA 19087-8640

Please add $1.75 for shipping and handling for the first book and $.50 for each book thereafter. NY, NYC, and PA residents, please add appropriate sales tax. No cash, stamps, or C.O.D.s. All orders shipped within 6 weeks via postal service book rate. Canadian orders require $2.00 extra postage and must be paid in U.S. dollars through a U.S. banking facility.

Name_____

Address_____

City_____ State_____ Zip_____

I have enclosed $_____ in payment for the checked book(s).

Payment <u>must</u> accompany all orders. ☐ Please send a free catalog.

CHECK OUT OUR WEBSITE! www.dorchesterpub.com

ZANE GREY

LAST OF
THE DUANES

Buck Duane's father was a gunfighter who died by the gun, and, in accepting a drunken bully's challenge, Duane finds himself forced into the life of an outlaw. He roams the dark trails of southwestern Texas, living in outlaw camps, until he meets the one woman who can help him overcome his past—a girl named Jennie Lee.

___4430-7 $4.99 US/$5.99 CAN

KIT CARSON

MOUNTAIN DEMON

DOUG HAWKINS

Kit Carson is legendary for his fighting skills. He can go toe to toe with any man and come out on top. But how can he beat an enemy that isn't human? When Kit finds himself snowbound in an isolated mountain cabin with only a few friends, he knows they are in for a hard time. But then they start to see signs that they aren't alone—and that whatever is out there in the snow isn't like anything they've seen before. Kit and his friends have all heard tales of the Wendigo, but can they survive meeting one face-to-face?

___4619-9 $3.99 US/$4.99 CAN

Last Chance

DEE MARVINE

Mattie Hamil is on a frantic journey west. On her own, with only her grit and determination to see her through, she has to find her charming gambler of a fiancé, and she has to do it fast—before her pregnancy shows. From a steamboat along the Missouri River to the rough-and-tumble post-gold-rush town of Last Chance, Montana, Mattie's trek leads her through danger and sorrow, friendship and joy. But even after she finds her fiancé, no bend in the trail leads to what she expected.

___4475-7 $4.99 US/$5.99 CAN

Dorchester Publishing Co., Inc.
P.O. Box 6640
Wayne, PA 19087-8640

Please add $1.75 for shipping and handling for the first book and $.50 for each book thereafter. NY, NYC, and PA residents, please add appropriate sales tax. No cash, stamps, or C.O.D.s. All orders shipped within 6 weeks via postal service book rate. Canadian orders require $2.00 extra postage and must be paid in U.S. dollars through a U.S. banking facility.

Name_____
Address_____
City_____State_____Zip_____
I have enclosed $_____ in payment for the checked book(s).
Payment <u>must</u> accompany all orders. ❑ Please send a free catalog.
       CHECK OUT OUR WEBSITE! www.dorchesterpub.com

BLOOD BROTHERS
GARY McCARTHY

Ben Pope and Rick Kilbane are as different as night and day. A miner's son, Ben is an awkward, earnest kid with no money and lots of hard luck. Rick is the wild, troublemaking son of Ulysses Kilbane, a professional gambler and the fastest gun on Nevada's Comstock Lode. But despite their differences, Ben and Rick have always been best friends and blood brothers. That may all change, though, now that Ben has pinned on a sheriff's badge. That tin star has set the blood brothers down the road to the ultimate showdown—a final test of friendship and loyalty. A test that one of them may not survive.

___4585-0 $3.99 US/$4.99 CAN

NOBILITY

TIM McGUIRE

Clay Cole is a man on the run for a crime he never committed. But it's getting harder to run when it seems like everywhere he goes people have heard of the man known as the Rainmaker. When a young boy saves Clay's life, Clay figures the only honorable thing to do is help the boy's mother in the vicious land battle she's part of—even if that means staying put for a while. But if he stops running long enough for the past to catch up with him, the Rainmaker may not have much of a future.

___4526-5 $4.50 US/$5.50 CAN

Dorchester Publishing Co., Inc.
P.O. Box 6640
Wayne, PA 19087-8640

Please add $1.75 for shipping and handling for the first book and $.50 for each book thereafter. NY, NYC, and PA residents, please add appropriate sales tax. No cash, stamps, or C.O.D.s. All orders shipped within 6 weeks via postal service book rate. Canadian orders require $2.00 extra postage and must be paid in U.S. dollars through a U.S. banking facility.

Name_____
Address_____
City_____State_____Zip_____
I have enclosed $_____ in payment for the checked book(s).
Payment <u>must</u> accompany all orders. ❑ Please send a free catalog.
    CHECK OUT OUR WEBSITE! www.dorchesterpub.com

John D. Nesbitt

Travis Quinn doesn't have much luck picking his friends. He is fired from the last ranch he works on when a friend of his gets blacklisted for going behind the owner's back. Guilt by association sends Quinn looking for another job, too. He makes his way down the Powder River country until he runs into Miles Newman, who puts in a good word for him and gets him a job at the Lockhart Ranch. But Quinn doesn't know too much about Newman, and the more he learns, the less he likes. Pretty soon it starts to look like Quinn has picked the wrong friend again. And if the rumors about Newman are true, this friend might just get him killed.

___4671-7 $4.50 US/$5.50 CAN

THE WHITE CHIP

NELSON C. NYE

The Lost Dutchman is the most fabled gold mine of the Old West. Hundreds of hopefuls have risked everything to find it—many never coming back. When an unlikely caravan finds the cleverly sealed-off entrance, the dizzying wealth is theirs for the taking—if they can retrieve it from the middle of an active volcano.

___4473-0 $4.50 US/$5.50 CAN

Dorchester Publishing Co., Inc.
P.O. Box 6640
Wayne, PA 19087-8640

Please add $1.75 for shipping and handling for the first book and $.50 for each book thereafter. NY, NYC, and PA residents, please add appropriate sales tax. No cash, stamps, or C.O.D.s. All orders shipped within 6 weeks via postal service book rate. Canadian orders require $2.00 extra postage and must be paid in U.S. dollars through a U.S. banking facility.

Name_____
Address_____
City_____State_____Zip_____
I have enclosed $_____ in payment for the checked book(s).
Payment <u>must</u> accompany all orders. ❑ Please send a free catalog.
CHECK OUT OUR WEBSITE! www.dorchesterpub.com

RATTLESNAKE

T.V. OLSEN

The Apache wars took almost everything from Indian Jim Izancho. Now Senator Warrender wants the one thing he has left—his land—and Warrender's Indian-hating son soon begins a reign of terror against the Izancho family. The only man who will try to save Jim is his boyhood friend, Sheriff Frank Tenney. Only Tenney can stop a deadly feud between a white man—who happens to be his father-in-law—and the Apache who once saved his life, a man who has been pushed too far and is now hell-bent on vengeance, a man as dangerous as a cornered rattlesnake.

___4620-2 $4.50 US/$5.50 CAN

DARK EMBERS AT DAWN
STEPHEN OVERHOLSER

Like many a veteran of the Civil War, Cap McKenna went west to the Rockies to build a new life. But that new life changes forever the day he comes across an abandoned infant, whom he takes in and cares for until the baby's Cheyenne mother appears at his door. Alone and terrified, all the woman wants is to find the baby's father. Cap helps her locate him at the U.S. Cavalry encampment, but Colonel Tom Sully stands defiantly between the father and his family. When the desperate man deserts to be with his wife and child, Sully sends a detail after him and suddenly Cap finds himself caught in a deadly pursuit—ready to risk all for what he knows is right.

___4657-1 $4.50 US/$5.50 CAN